Become a tycoon, he'd said.

By the time she reached home, Piper Duchess had made up her mind. She would throw herself into work. She would become a millionaire *before* she was thirty.

That would prove to Nic de Pastrana that she didn't need *him*.

But that was before Nic turned up on her doorstep—needing her help....

THE HUSBAND FUND trilogy
by Rebecca Winters
Only in Harlequin Romance®!

Book 1—*To Catch a Groom* (#3819)
Book 2—*To Win His Heart* (#3827)
Book 3—*To Marry for Duty* (#3835)

Dear Reader,

I came from a family of five sisters and one brother. The four oldest girls were my parents' first family. There was a space before my baby sister and baby brother came along.

My mother called the first four her little women, and gave each of us a Madame Alexander doll from the *Little Women* series based on the famous book by Louisa May Alcott. We may not have been quadruplets, but we were close in age and definitely felt a connection to each other that often meant we tuned into each others' thoughts as we sang, played, studied and traveled together.

In our early twenties I recall a time when I took the train from Paris, France, where I'd been studying, to meet one of my sisters at the port in Genoa, Italy, where her ship came in from New York. She was returning to school in Perugia, Italy. Some of my choicest memories are our glorious adventures as two blond American sisters on vacation along the French and Italian rivieras, dodging Mediterranean playboys.

When I conceived *The Husband Fund* trilogy for Harlequin Romance®, I have no doubt the idea of triplet sisters coming to Europe on a lark to intentionally meet some gorgeous Riviera playboys sprang to life from my own family experiences at home and abroad.

Meet Greer, Olivia and Piper, three characters drawn from my imagination who probably have traits from all four of my wonderful, intelligent, talented sisters in their makeup.

Enjoy!

Rebecca Winters

www.rebeccawinters-author.com

TO MARRY FOR DUTY

Rebecca Winters

The
HUSBAND
FUND

HARLEQUIN®

TORONTO • NEW YORK • LONDON
AMSTERDAM • PARIS • SYDNEY • HAMBURG
STOCKHOLM • ATHENS • TOKYO • MILAN • MADRID
PRAGUE • WARSAW • BUDAPEST • AUCKLAND

ISBN 0-373-03835-6

TO MARRY FOR DUTY

First North American Publication 2005.

This edition published by arrangement with Harlequin Books S.A.

www.eHarlequin.com

Printed in U.S.A.

CHAPTER ONE

August
Kingston, New York

"THANKS for seeing me on such short notice, Dr. Arnavitz. I've never been to a psychiatrist before, so I'm nervous."

He cocked his gray head. "Nervousness on the part of my patients seems to go with the territory. At least on a first visit. Why don't you tell me what's bothering you and we'll start there."

Piper Duchess sat on the edge of the chair with her hands rigidly clasped on top of her knees. "Everything's bothering me—" she blurted before hot tears rolled down her flushed cheeks.

Without saying anything the doctor pushed a box of tissues toward her. She took one and wiped the moisture from her face. When she'd regained a little composure, she said, "For the first time in my life, I'm really alone, and I'm not handling it very well. To be honest, I'm not handling it at all—" She broke down again.

"Do you mean emotionally, physically?"

"Both." She blotted her aqua eyes with another tissue.

"From your chart I see that you're twenty-seven years old and single. Are you going through a breakup with a boyfriend or fiancé?"

No.

Nic didn't qualify for either category and anyway he wasn't interested in her. In fact Nicolas de Pastrana of the House of Parma-Bourbon in Spain had always been off limits to her though she hadn't known that when she'd first met him and his cousins.

"No," her voice trembled, "but I would imagine this is exactly how it must feel. No wonder it's such a traumatic experience."

"Tell me about your family."

"My parents have both passed away. My sisters Greer and Olivia are now married and live in Europe. Olivia just got married in Marbella. I flew home from Spain to New York three days ago."

"You live alone?"

She nodded. "In a basement apartment here in Kingston. The three of us shared it after Daddy died in the spring."

"You have no extended family?"

"No. Our parents were both older when they married and their families have all passed on."

"So you're virtually alone now."

Her throat started to close up with pain. "Yes. I sound like a big baby, don't I?"

"Not at all. Most people have some relatives living in the same country at least. Where do you fit in your family constellation?"

Piper thought she understood what he meant. "I'm the middle child, but that may sound misleading since my sisters and I are nonidentical triplets."

"Ah…" That was all he said, but apparently it answered some questions for him.

"I've never been completely alone like this before.

I'm not talking just the physical separation from my sisters. It's a mental thing.''

''The reign of the Three Musketeers has come to an end?'' he supplied.

''Yes!'' she cried. ''It's exactly like that. All for one, one for all. Now they have husbands and nothing will ever be the same again.''

''Are you angry about that?''

Her head was bowed. ''Yes. I know that's an awful thing to say.''

''You're wrong. It's the honest thing to say. If you'd said anything else, I wouldn't have believed you.''

''It's my fault they're married, so I don't have anyone to blame but myself.''

''You mean you held a gun to their husbands' heads when they proposed to your sisters?''

She laughed in spite of her tears. If only he knew the extent of the machinations involved. ''No.''

''So how could their marriages be your fault?''

''It's a long story.''

''We have twenty more minutes.''

Meaning she'd better get to the point fast. ''Greer's the oldest. She always told Olivia and me what to do. She was the one who talked us into starting our Internet business after college. It was her plan that we become millionaires by the time we were thirty, so she said none of us could get married or it would spoil everything.

''Olivia and I didn't care about becoming millionaires and figured we needed to get her married off first so we could meet a man and settle down to be happy like our parents.

"Dad worried about Greer's attitude too. Before he died, Olivia and I came up with a plan for him to leave any money to us in a special fund we called the Husband Fund.

"The one legal stipulation was that we could only use the money to find a husband, and for no other reason. Of course Daddy, who approved of the idea wholeheartedly, didn't let on to Greer that we were behind it.

"In June we planned a trip to the Riviera, the perfect place for all of us to meet an exciting man. The whole point was for Greer to meet one who would cause her to forget about becoming a millionaire.

"Greer went along with it because she was carrying out Daddy's last wish. But she had no intention of getting married, only of getting a playboy to propose to her while we were on vacation. Then she would turn him down flat for the sheer fun of it.

"We pretended to go along with her plan. Then to our amazement she met Maximilliano di Varano of the House of Parma-Bourbon, the man of her dreams, and she ended up proposing to him! They were married inside of six weeks, and now live in Italy.

"That was terrific. It meant Olivia and I could go back to New York and do our own thing. But then," her voice shook, "Olivia fell in love with Max's first cousin, Lucien de Falcon, also of the House of Parma-Bourbon. They were just married a few days ago and will be living in Monaco."

The doctor nodded. "So now you're free to do your own thing."

A sob got trapped in her throat. *My own thing.* "I don't know what that is anymore."

Dr. Arnavitz sat forward. "The end of the Three Musketeers may be the end of your girlhood, but it's the beginning of Piper Duchess's life as a woman with new worlds to conquer. Europe is as near as the next plane ride."

"I know," she said in a dull voice.

But Nic was there. After the way he'd rejected her, she refused to give him the satisfaction of thinking she was aware of his existence.

"Are you still working at your Internet business?"

"Yes."

"Tell me about it."

"I'm an artist. I draw illustrations for wall calendars with slogans that appeal to women. You know like, 'If you need to get it done, ask a woman.' Greer thought up the slogans, and Olivia did the marketing."

He smiled. "Does it provide you with a good living?"

"Yes. They're selling well throughout the U.S. and are going to be distributed in a couple of cities in Europe."

"Lucky you. Why don't you turn the tables on Greer?"

"What do you mean?"

"Your sister wanted to be a millionaire by the time she was thirty. You wanted to get married. So get busy seeing how much money *you* can make by the time you're thirty.

"Broaden your horizons. There's always South America, Australia, the Far East. Set up office space. Hire staff. Become a tycoon. Make it into an empire. Who knows what the future holds in store for you?

"If you stay in that basement apartment and remain

angry, no one will feel sorry for you. Not every woman has your intelligence, your talent, your health, your lovely blond looks, your ability to do whatever you want. There's nothing to stop you except your own unhealthy self-pity.''

Ooh.

Dr. Arnavitz knew how to hit where it hurt. But that's what she was paying him $200.00 a half hour for.

Speaking of half hour, her time was up. She thanked him for seeing her and told him she'd think hard about what he'd said.

On the drive back to the apartment in her dad's old Pontiac, the doctor's admonition kept swirling around in her head.

Become a tycoon, he'd said. Hire staff.

By the time she reached home, she'd made up her mind that she would become a millionaire *before* she was thirty. It would prove to Nic she didn't need *him*.

The second she got back to her apartment, she marched into the living room which she and the girls had turned into an office, and phoned Don Jardine. He was Greer's former boyfriend, the man who'd never stood a chance with her. It was Don who owned and ran the company that printed the calendars they sold and distributed throughout the States.

''Hi, Don!''

''Piper— I didn't realize you were back from Europe. How did everything go?''

She noticed he didn't ask about Greer. Smart man. Piper planned to take a leaf out of his book and never ask her sisters about Nic.

''Olivia is now married to Lucien de Falcon. That's

how things went! I'll let you be the one to tell Fred the news.''

Fred was Olivia's former boyfriend, and Don's friend.

After a prolonged silence, ''That's two down. There must be something in the Varano genes that's fatal for the Duchess triplets.''

Don must have been reading Piper's mind. No doubt there was a scientific explanation for the fact that she and her sisters were all enamored of men who belonged to the same family.

Once she read about two male twins in England who fell in love with the same woman. She loved them both, so the three of them settled down together and lived happily ever after. At the time Piper read the story to her sisters, all three of them rolled on the floor with laughter, but Piper wasn't rolling with laughter now.

''Not this Duchess triplet!'' she declared with vehemence.

''Does that mean there's hope for Tom after all?''

''No.''

Tom was Piper's ex-boyfriend and another good friend of Don's. Once upon a time all six of them had enjoyed waterskiing and going to movies in a group. As Greer had always pointed out, there was safety in numbers.

Truer words were never spoken. Once Max had gotten Greer to himself, that was the end of the girls' lifelong triumvirate. It started the domino effect. Olivia fell under Luc's spell. As for Piper...

Piper was a fool who would never, ever throw herself at a man again.

"I have a business proposition for you. It's big."

"How big?"

"Want to fly to Sydney, Tokyo and Rio with me to find out? Depending on the outcome, we'll incorporate and offer shares on the stock market. Are you interested?"

A long silence ensued. "How soon do you want to get together to talk?"

"Tonight if you're free. First off we need to come up with the best savvy corporate attorney we can find."

"Agreed. But what about Europe?"

Her body stiffened. "Forget it. I'm never stepping foot on that continent again."

"You don't mean that, Piper. Your sisters live there."

"Then they'll have to come to me if they want to see me."

"What am I missing here? I thought garnering new markets was the reason you were in Spain last week."

"I thought so too until I found out it was a setup. I really don't want to talk about it."

"If you want me for a business partner, I'm afraid you're going to have to. How were you set up, and more importantly, why?"

Still bristling with rage Piper said, "The Varano cousins used their powerful influence and money to pay Signore Tozetti to be our European distributor.

"It was a clever move on Luc's part. He lured Olivia back to Europe through a lucrative business offer so he could win her forgiveness for his utter cruelty to her. His cunning plan worked so well, they are now on their honeymoon!

"But I don't want any part of the money our calendars might make over there. We didn't win that contract from Signore Tozetti on the merits of our talents alone."

Piper would divide any profits made in Europe between her sisters. She didn't plan on keeping a penny of the money Nic had anything to do with!

"I can't say I blame you for that," Don murmured.

"Thank you for understanding."

"I understand a lot more than you think. You're the artist after all. A brilliant one I might add."

"Thanks, Don."

"It's true. One day you're going to be famous, Piper."

That's what Olivia had said before they'd both found out they'd been set up.

Mother and Daddy would be so proud to know your drawings are going to be famous all over Europe, Piper.

We don't know that yet, so let's not count our chickens.

Signore Tozetti wouldn't have paid us an advance to come to Spain if he didn't believe he was going to make a bundle off you pretty soon. When he sees what you've done in just three days, he'll be sending you everywhere; France— Switzerland—

Her hand tightened on the phone receiver. "You don't become famous with a bunch of calendars."

"Your calendars have only been a stepping stone. It's time to branch out."

He was starting to sound like Dr. Arnavitz. "In what way?"

"Commercial advertising over television and the

Internet is hot. Think global and the sky's the limit. Megacorporations spanning several continents pay seven and eight digit figures to the artist who can come up with the right worldwide image.''

She blinked. ''How long have you been thinking this big for me?''

''Ever since I started printing the calendars for Duchesse Designs. You've got that touch of genius, Piper. Maybe with my help we can ignite it.''

''I like the way you think. Can you come over at seven?''

''I'll be there with some ideas that have been percolating for a long time.''

''Did you ever tell Greer about this?''

''What do you think?''

''You're right. That was sort of a dumb question.''

No one ever told Greer anything except Max. He'd managed to kiss her senseless on the *Piccione,* have her arrested and put in an Italian jail for the night, after which he'd propositioned her. It was the perfect path to her heart, and she'd ended up throwing herself at him.

Luc had operated a little differently. After breaking Olivia's heart because of a tragic misunderstanding, he'd gotten her back to Europe on false pretenses. Then he'd locked her inside a robot-limo he'd designed and named Cog. It had so many clever inventions to break down her defenses, Olivia had practically crumbled on the spot forgiving him.

It was sickening.

Piper was happy for the four of them. She really was, but she didn't want to think about her brothers-in-law, or she would start thinking about Nic, and that kind of thinking was disastrous.

January 26
Marbella, Spain

"Señor Pastrana?"

"Sí, Filomena?"

Nic was on the verge of leaving his office at the Banco De Iberia. Since he'd restructured its branch network, the bank had enjoyed another successful financial quarter that exceeded his expectations, but he took no joy in it.

"A gentleman is on the phone for you from Christie's auction house in New York." At the mere mention of New York, Nic's pulse rate suddenly tripled. "Shall I put him through, or do you want me to take a message?"

"I'll speak to him now."

"Very good, Señor."

While he waited, he closed the file on the bank's foreign gold reserves he'd been examining and turned off the computer.

"Señor Pastrana?" an American sounding voice came over the speakerphone.

"This is he. Go ahead."

"John Vashom here from the fine jewels department at Christie's. Since you first alerted us, we've been watching for any jewelry from the Marie-Louise collection stolen from the Varano family palace in Colorno, Italy.

"This morning a jeweled comb showed up for auction by an anonymous seller. I went to our jewel loss register database and pulled out the pictures you supplied us. The piece in question appears to be a perfect match. How would you like me to proceed?''

An adrenaline rush drove Nic to his feet.

By some miracle he'd just been handed the legitimate excuse that would take him to New York, thereby getting him out of the final hellish commitment to the family of his deceased fiancée Nina Robles. The dreaded monthly duty visit wouldn't be happening after all. Indeed, never again.

''I appreciate your quick handling of the matter, Mr. Vashom.''

''I try to do my best.''

Without conscious thought Nic pulled the black mourning band off his arm and tossed it in the wastebasket. It was a struggle for him to contain his excitement. ''An agent from the CIA will be contacting you within the hour. In the meantime, hold on to the comb and say nothing to anyone.''

''You can count on me.''

Nic checked his watch. It was nine-thirty in the morning on the East Coast of the U.S. ''I'm on my way to New York now. Expect me before your closing time. I'll need your cell phone number so we can stay in touch.''

While he wrote it down, his mind made a mental list of people to call. The second they hung up, he phoned the chief investigator in Rome coordinating the efforts of the various police and undercover agents working on the case. Signore Barzini would contact the CIA in New York.

Next he called Signore Rossi, Italy's top jewelry authenticator, and arranged for him to fly to New York from Parma in one of the Varano jets. Only he could declare if the jeweled comb was the genuine article.

The collection had belonged to the Duchess of Parma, otherwise known as Marie-Louise of Austria of the House of Bourbon, second wife of Napoleon Bonaparte. The theft of the treasure almost two years earlier had been a blow to the whole family. Since that time Nic and his cousins had been conducting an international investigation with the help of police and undercover agents.

One authenticated piece had been recovered when it turned up at a London auction last August. He'd paid a small fortune to get it back. Unfortunately there'd been no leads on the person or persons responsible for the daring jewelry heist.

Now that another part of the collection had shown up in the States, perhaps a fake, perhaps not, Nic was hopeful for a break in the case.

He rang his father but got his voice mail. After apprising him of the situation, he asked his parent to make his excuses to the Robles family for not being able to join them. Even Nic's father would agree that the call from the auction house constituted the kind of emergency over which Nina's parents couldn't take exception.

The Pastrana and the Robles family shared ties through the Spanish House of Bourbon that ran deep. However if Nina's parents believed they could foist their twenty-seven-year-old daughter Camilla on Nic as a replacement for Nina because of some ancient family custom, then they were more out of touch with reality than he'd first supposed.

After summoning his driver, Nic left the bank

through his private entrance and climbed in the back of the limo. En route to the airport he phoned the pilot and told him to get the Pastrana jet ready. There was no need to stop by the villa. Nic kept a change of clothes and toiletries on board.

Euphoric to have thrown off the shackles of his bondage, he phoned Max to fill him in on everything, but he got his cousin's voice mail as well. Frustrated not to be able to talk to him, he left a message about his plans, then called Luc who picked up on the third ring.

"Olivia and I were just about to call you. We're sailing to Mallorca this weekend. How would you like to join us there on Sunday after you're through with your duty visit?"

Luc sounded like a different man these days. Since his marriage to Olivia, he was beyond happy. They were expecting a baby in September. Nic had never known a more ecstatic couple except for Max and Greer who'd put in for adoption and were waiting.

"There's nothing I'd like more, but something important has come up. I have news that can't wait." Within minutes he'd told him about the phone call from Christie's.

In an instant Luc's mood had sobered. "I'll meet you in New York."

"No. You and Olivia need your time alone. I'm only telling you this because I'll be gone a while following the investigation."

"What's going on?"

Nic took a fortifying breath. "What if I told you the arm band is sitting in the wastebasket of my office getting ready to be tossed out with the trash in the next few minutes?''

''*¡Dieu merci!*'' his cousin exploded. ''It was an archaic custom you should never have been subjected to. I hope this means what I think it means.''

''It's all I've been able to think about since Max's wedding,'' he whispered.

''You may have problems tracking Piper down. She called Olivia from Sydney last week. I'm not sure if she's back in the States yet.''

''I'll find her, even if I have to fly to Australia.''

''Should I hear anything different, I'll let you know. Are you sure you don't want me to come to New York?''

''Let's wait and see what Signore Rossi has to say about the comb. If it's the original, then we'll have a confab with Max.''

''All right. Take care and good luck, *mon vieux*.''

Nic knew what his cousin meant. Since Luc's wedding, Nic hadn't laid eyes on Piper. Because of the hated black band, a grim reminder of his dark past with all its attendant pain, he hadn't been able to do anything about her.

For the last eleven months, twenty-five days and seven hours, he'd worn the band faithfully...except for a four day period last June when he'd taken it off to go undercover as the captain of the *Piccione*.

Those four days had been long enough for him to have become bewitched by a pair of aquamarine eyes shot with blue while he and his cousins pursued the Duchess triplets, believing them to be the thieves responsible for the stolen jewels from the Varano family palace in Colorno, Italy.

Nothing could have been further from the truth, and in that short period of time his life had changed forever.

"I'm going to need it, Luc."

"What's your plan?"

"That's a good question. Technically speaking I should have waited another week before removing the band. But since I'm leaving the country for an indeterminate period, no one's going to know the difference except Piper. That is if she's still speaking to me."

"If anyone can win her around, you can. Talk to you later."

"I'll let you know when I've made contact," he said with more confidence than he felt. Nic wasn't certain of anything where she was concerned. All he knew was that he felt out of breath just anticipating seeing her again.

Now that he'd brought his period of mourning to a close, nothing and no one was going to stand in the way of his getting what he wanted...

January 29
Kingston, New York

"Excuse me for interrupting, Piper, but there's a man out in front who's asking for you."

Jan, the former northeast distributor for Duchesse Designs was now Piper's assistant in the company she'd formed with Don Jardine. They'd ended up calling it Cyber Network Concepts.

Piper kept sketching at her drafting table. "I'm not officially in until tomorrow."

She'd moved into the Jardine office building where Don still ran his printing business on the side. He'd given her the suite next to him with a connecting door. So far the arrangement had been working perfectly.

"I told him that, but he insists on seeing you anyway."

"What's his name?"

"He said he preferred to surprise you."

"That's a pushy salesman tactic. He's probably the regional manager from Mid Valley machines. They've been pestering us to buy their products for months. Get rid of him, Jan."

"He warned me he wouldn't leave until he'd spoken to you. I'm afraid he means it."

"They *all* mean it. If he's so anxious, tell him to talk to Don."

"He doesn't want to talk to him."

"Then he's wasting our time. If he were a client, he would have told you his name. Since we've paid all our bills, he couldn't be a creditor. Tell him we just got back from Sydney with a ton of work to do. Tomorrow's Tuesday. I'll see him then."

In the last six months she and Don had already garnered four lucrative advertising accounts with American companies doing business in Australia and South America. Piper had more work than she could handle now.

"I'm afraid he's not going to take no for an answer."

A certain nuance in her voice brought Piper's head around. Bringing Jan in as office manager and head of their calendar sales in the U.S. had been a master stroke. Because Jan had great business sense, Piper was surprised to discover that her recently engaged assistant could be intimidated by anyone.

"How come you're afraid to tell him no?"

"He has an aura about him. You know…a certain presence, probably because he's foreign."

The hairs prickled on the back of Piper's neck. "How foreign?"

"If you're talking about his English, he speaks it perfectly with a slight accent. I think he might be a Mediterranean type or something close to it."

"So he's dark-haired?"

"Yes. But tall and…well…you know…built like you wish all guys were built if you know what I mean. To be honest, he's the most attractive male I've ever met in my life. Please don't tell Jim what I said—"

The charcoal slipped from Piper's fingers. Three men fit that description. They all belonged to the same family.

"Did this man's accent sound French?"

"I wouldn't know."

"Are his eyes a fiery black?"

"No. They're a piercing brown."

Help!

Piper tried to swallow. It was impossible. "Is he wearing an arm band?"

"A what?"

"A black arm band above the elbow to designate he's in mourning?"

"No. He's dressed in this fabulous stone gray suit. I know this might sound weird to you, but he carries himself like he's…royalty."

Piper jumped up from her drafting table in shock. "Jan? You've just met the future Duc de Pastrana of the House of Parma-Bourbon. Nic is the first cousin of Greer and Olivia's husbands." No wonder Jan acted as if she'd just been through a life-changing experience. In an absolute panic she continued.

"If you value your job, you'll let me put your engagement ring on. I only need it for a few minutes. Until he leaves I'm not just Don's business partner, I'm his fiancée! Have you got that?"

Her assistant slowly nodded before removing her modest diamond ring. Piper slipped it on. It was a little loose because Jan was larger boned, but it didn't matter. It was an engagement ring and would do the job.

"Thank you. For this favor you'll get a bonus in your next paycheck. Go ahead and send him back."

Piper's heart thundered beneath the navy pullover she'd slipped on with her jeans earlier that morning. When she wasn't traveling to meet with clients, she hibernated in her office to do her artwork away from people.

She sat down at her desk, then stood up again, trying to decide how she would greet him. When she caught sight of his tall, striking physique in the doorway, she'd just sat down again which was a good thing. Her legs wouldn't have supported her.

"Well, well, well," she declared with feigned nonchalance, taking the offensive. "If it isn't the captain of the *Piccione*."

CHAPTER TWO

"BUENOS dias, Señorita Piperre."

When Nic rolled the "r" that way, Piper felt it resonate through every particle of her body. No matter how hard she tried to harden herself against his potent male presence, she failed.

"The last time I saw you, you were hiding in the bushes on your estate, waiting to spirit me away so Luc could do his worst to Olivia."

At the time she'd hoped Nic had forgotten about his mourning period and would do his worst to *her*. After all, he'd removed the mourning band for a short while on the *Piccione*. Piper had been dying for him to kiss her.

Instead he'd led her to the family chapel with the priest in attendance. That's where she'd found Greer and Max, in fact the whole Parma-Bourbon family, waiting to observe the imminent nuptials of the youngest Duchess triplet and the oldest son of the Duc de Falcon.

Nic must have been remembering that night too. He flashed her what she and her sisters called his Castilian smile, a dazzling white masculine smile that was his unique signature.

But as he'd once explained, Castilian was a misnomer since the Varano part of him was Italian, and the Pastrana side of him didn't come from Castile. The

Pastrana's royal roots lay in that southern region of Spain known as Andalusia.

Through Piper's sisters she'd learned that the Robles family also claimed a royal connection through the Spanish House of Bourbon, but never gained the Pastrana's prominence.

"How come you're slumming it in American waters? Has some urgent business brought you to the other side of the Atlantic?"

He lifted his proud, aristocratic head and shot her an enigmatic glance. She thought he looked leaner, a little more drawn, yet he was more gorgeous than ever. Piper wasn't the type to faint, but if she were, she'd be lying flat as a pancake on the floor of her office!

"I've been in New York for the last few days because another piece of jewelry from the stolen collection showed up at Christie's auction house. It turned out to be authentic."

"Don't tell me the Duchesse pendant has been unearthed at last?"

"No. A jeweled comb."

Piper had forgotten all about the collection. If she and her sisters hadn't worn their own Duchesse pendants to Italy on their first trip, they would never have known about the museum theft of another pendant identical to theirs, or have become involved with the three cousins.

She would never have met Nicolas de Pastrana.

No matter that he'd crushed her heart, the thought of not knowing him was so incomprehensible, she shivered.

Furious at her involuntary reaction to him she said, "If by any chance my sisters suggested you drop by here to persuade me to fly to Europe for a visit, you've wasted your precious time.''

He stood with his legs slightly apart, his strong tanned hands clasped in front of him. ''Your sisters have no idea I'm here.''

She flashed him her arctic smile. ''Since your period of mourning isn't up until February, I'll wager Nina's family doesn't know you're here either.''

Piper had purposely introduced his dead fiancée's name to remind him of the way he'd rejected her advances to him that hot afternoon after Max's wedding.

When she'd tried to help him remove his tuxedo jacket and suggested they take a little nap in the grass by the old water wheel to cool off, he'd pushed her hands away.

After mocking her because she didn't know how to behave in polite society with a man wearing a mourning band, he'd said he would excuse it on the grounds that she was one of the notorious Duchess triplets.

The hurt he'd inflicted would never go away. She would never forgive him.

He must have been reading her mind because he removed his suit jacket with effortless male grace, drawing her attention to the breadth of his shoulders. There was no band on the outside of his dove gray shirtsleeve either.

''As you can see, I'm no longer in mourning.''

''Don't tell me— You had other business in New York, so you removed your arm band early. It couldn't be because you've decided you're ready to lie down and take that nap with me before you fly back to Marbella, could it?'' She eyed him narrowly. ''In my neck of the woods, that's called *cheating*. It's something I don't do.''

Lines darkened Nic's rugged features. Good. She'd hit a nerve, and she would go on pressing against it until she got rid of him.

''I've come to ask an important favor of you,'' his voice grated.

''Really.'' Flame licked her cheeks. ''Does Nina's sister Camilla know about this? I understand she's waiting in the wings until next month when she expects to become your new fiancée.''

A tiny nerve throbbed along the ridge of Nic's taut patrician jaw. It had to frustrate him that nothing in his personal life was sacred now that his cousins were married to her sisters.

''I'm here to talk about us.''

''Us?'' she exploded. ''There is no *us!* I got engaged in Sydney and know enough about polite society to play around with my own fiancé and no one else.''

A stunning stillness pervaded the atmosphere. Nic's eyes narrowed to slits. ''I don't believe you.''

Her heart almost palpitated out of her chest. ''What don't you believe? That I have principles? Or that I'm an engaged woman now?''

Enjoying this triumphant moment, she buzzed Don. It was a huge risk to take, but he knew all about her broken heart. She was depending on him to play along.

''Don?''

''Hi. I was just about to ask if you want to go to lunch at Alfie's.''

Don got A-plus for that opening.

''I'd love it! First though, can you come in my office for a minute? We have a visitor from Spain, Nicolas de Pastrana, Greer's and Olivia's cousin. He's here to ask me a favor. Since you and I got engaged in Sydney, I'd like the two of you to meet."

"I'll be right there," Don said without missing a heartbeat. Bless the man.

The second her business partner breezed through the connecting door, Piper gravitated toward him and was given a loving hug. She looked up at him. "Honey? I was just telling Nic our news."

As she turned to Nic, she purposely exposed her left hand for him to view the ring. A thrill of alarm passed through her body to see his fierce expression, showing a hint of the Mediterranean fire that flowed through his Andalusian veins.

"This is my fiancé, Don Jardine."

Nic nodded to Don, not making an effort to shake his hand. "Jardine—weren't you once involved with Greer?"

Piper reeled for a moment.

"We dated."

At Don's brief reply, Nic's lips twisted in distaste before he impaled her with his dark, penetrating gaze. "All for one, and one for all. The Duchess motto," his deep voice trailed.

Before she could credit it, he'd reached for her left hand. "A very nice ring, but it's a little loose isn't it?" With the agility of a magician he slipped it from her finger and lifted it to eye level for examination. "To Jan forever," he read the inscription aloud.

Don gave Piper's waist a "good luck, you'll need it" squeeze before retreating to his office. Once she heard the click of the door Nic said, "He's a pushover for the Duchesses of Kingston. I actually feel sorry for him.''

She stiffened. ''That was a cruel thing for you to do in front of him.''

''No crueler than you asking your assistant to relinquish her ring because you're the boss. I noticed it on her finger while she waited on me at the front desk.'' He made a fist around it and put it in his pocket.

Piper might have known his eagle eye would catch her out in her blatant lie. Nothing got past him. ''You've missed your calling as an undercover agent.''

''I was just going to say the same thing about you. More than ever I'm convinced you're the only person who can help me.''

She let out an angry laugh and the movement caused the fine gold strands of her hair to settle around her jawline. ''I bet Camilla doesn't have a clue you've made this side trip to Kingston to dally with the last unattached, *notorious* Duchess triplet.''

''Camilla and her family will know soon enough,'' the cryptic words dropped like icicles off a roof.

Though she was trembling with conflicting emotions, she would rather die than let him know it. ''What's that supposed to mean?''

''I need your assistance. It's important.''

''You said that before.''

''I'll make it worth your while.''

''If you're talking money, forget it. You and your cousins may have bribed Signore Tozetti to lure Olivia back to Europe, but that kind of charade only works once. Don and I have our own business enterprise now. I prefer to earn my money the old-fashioned way."

He moved closer, making it difficult for her to function or breathe. "I was thinking more along the lines of a baby."

"A baby—"

"Yes. Both your sisters are expecting one in the near future. You could be too…"

Piper blinked in shock, trying desperately to connect the dots. What on earth was he getting at?

"If you're insinuating I've been sleeping with Don, then you're way off base! In the first place, neither of us has ever been interested in each other that way, and we would *never* do that to Greer.

"In the second place, if I were expecting Don's baby, I certainly wouldn't need your money. I'm doing just fine on my own."

His sensual mouth broke into a condescending smile. "I've already satisfied myself about you and Jardine. I was thinking in terms of *my* giving *you* a baby."

Piper couldn't possibly have heard him correctly. "Why in the world would you think I want a baby, let alone yours?"

"Because I was in Luc's office the day Olivia called you with her news. The speakerphone happened to be on." Piper's heartbeat picked up speed while she tried to recall her exact words. "The second your sister told you, you broke down in tears of happiness for her, then you said you thought she was the luckiest woman in the world."

"Of course I said that!" Piper defended in the steadiest voice she could muster. "Olivia was fortunate enough to fall in love with a man who loved her and wanted to marry her. It's the only way I would want to have a baby. By now you ought to know the Duchess sisters don't sleep around.''

He cocked his dark head. ''Once upon a time you invited me to take a nap in the grass with *you*.''

She gave him a fatuous smile. ''That was different. I didn't intend to sleep with you in the way you're thinking. I was only having a little fun with you because I didn't really believe you were in true mourning. Otherwise you would never have removed the band, not even to go undercover.''

Caught up in her emotions, she kept on talking faster and faster. ''Since my purpose for being in Europe was to win a proposal from a Riviera playboy, then throw it back in his face, I decided to see if I could kiss one out of you for the sheer challenge of it.

''But it seems I underestimated your love for your deceased fiancée after all.'' She shrugged her shoulders. ''In any event none of it matters because it's water in another ocean now.''

Shadows darkened his handsome face. ''Not quite. Your instincts were right the first time. I never loved Nina Robles.''

Piper couldn't be positive, but it sounded like he was telling the truth. She suspected that if he'd really been in love with Nina, he would have married her years before.

''So you wore the arm band a whole year to do penance for your sin?'' she taunted.

''Yes,'' came the surprisingly fierce rejoinder.

''Oh I see—'' She flashed him another mocking smile. ''Because you were born a royal, you were forced to enter into a loveless engagement and keep up the pretense. Poor Nicolas. In fairness to you, I don't suppose most royal engagements are true love matches.''

''Some are,'' he responded in a silky tone. ''In my case the situation was complicated because my family and the Robles family are distantly related and have been very close over the years. A marriage between Nina and me was expected.

''Her untimely death has complicated things further because Señor Robles expects me to marry Camilla according to an old law.''

''Sounds Biblical to me.''

''That's because it is,'' he muttered. ''My father is leaning heavily in that direction too.''

''So Camilla doesn't appeal to you either?''

''No. I'm in love with someone else, but I can't do anything about that because she's not in love with me.''

Nic's interest in another woman had to be the Parma-Bourbon's best kept secret, otherwise her sisters would have heard about it. The devastating revelation drove Piper to her desk where she sat down before pain caused her to disintegrate right in front of him. He was so out of her reach.

In a wooden voice she said, ''Why are you really here, Nic?''

''My official mourning period is over in three days. In order to foil both families' future plans for me, I would like to arrive back in Marbella with a wife.''

''A wife, huh? Well you shouldn't have any trouble. There must be a dozen eligible royal females who've had their eye on you for years.''

"None of them will do for what I have in mind. You're the one titleless woman I could bring home that my family won't be able to take exception to publicly, or ask me to renounce."

"You mean I'm tolerable because my sisters are married to your cousins, therefore *I* win the prize by default?" she cried out, her face red hot.

"That's part of it," he came back quietly. "My parents have met you and find you charming. They know the history of the Duchess sisters, and are aware you and I have spent time together on two different occasions during my mourning perio—"

"Wait a minute," she broke in. At this point she was so beside herself with anguish, she jumped to her feet again, then had to hold on to the edge of the desk for support. "That talk about a baby—you're not suggesting we pretend we've been seeing each other on the sly, and now I'm pregnant with your—"

"There'd be no pretense if we got married and had a short honeymoon on our way back to Spain," he interrupted. "By then we could tell the family it's possible we're expecting. That would make my marriage a *fait accompli* in every sense of the word."

She shook her head. "No way— The favor you're asking of me is impossible. Aside from the fact that I don't like you, you're in love with someone else!"

"Does that have to matter?"

His cold-blooded response left Piper nonplussed. "Obviously not to you, but it does to me. We're not in love with each other, so it wouldn't work. *Furthermore* I like my world just as it is. My career has taken off and I'm excited to see where it leads.

"Personally I can't conceive of anything more absurd than the two of us parading around as man and wife in a loveless union just because you want to pull some stunt to get out of marrying Camilla, and I'm the nearest available pawn.''

After a period of uncomfortable quiet he said, ''I understand how you feel.'' His benign response managed to infuriate her even more. ''My apologies for having asked something of you that is pure selfishness on my part and could even be dangerous. I won't disturb you again.''

With one of those barely discernible yet imperious bows which was second nature to him, he started for the door.

That did it.

''Oh no you don't!'' She ran ahead of him and put her back to the door so he couldn't leave. ''You don't drop a little bomb like that and then just walk out of here while I stagger around like a victim of shell-shock.''

Trying to catch her breath, she thought she detected a faint smile of satisfaction on his lips. Since he'd always found her amusing, she ought to be used to those horrible, patronizing looks he gave her. Unfortunately he'd only enflamed her.

She put her hands on her hips. ''I knew there had to be some other reason you came all this way to see me. Explain dangerous. To whom?''

''To both of us. Naturally I'd provide security so no harm would ever come to you.''

Hairs prickled on the back of her neck once more. ''Security?'' Despite her bravado, the sudden oblique expression in his eyes gave rise to an uneasy feeling inside her.

"A necessary precaution," he answered solemnly, trapping her eyes with his dark brown gaze. "But it's a moot point now. Rest assured that if you had agreed to become my wife, you would have been helping the entire family. In time you would have known the full gratitude of the House of Parma-Bourbon."

"I don't want anyone's gratitude!" Piper practically spit out the words. She wanted Nic's love, but that wasn't possible.

"Forgive me for having taken up your valuable time, Señorita Piperre." He shrugged back into his elegant suit jacket. "I'll let myself out."

As he reached past her to open the door, their arms brushed, sending a current of electricity through her body. Her pain flew off the chart.

"Be sure to give Jan back her ring before you leave the building," she cautioned in a brittle voice.

He paused in the entry, eyeing her through veiled lids. "But of course."

But of course nothing!

Her eyes prickled behind their lids. She glared at the door he'd closed on his way out.

How dare he have the gall to invade her space like some arrogant Spanish nobleman from the past, expecting her to fall for his *droit de seigneur* routine with its own peculiar Pastrana twist.

Dangerous my foot!

Wild with hurt, she wheeled around and poked her head inside Don's office. He looked up at her. "Something tells me I'm about to lose my business partner. Like I said, those Varano genes are fatal for the Duchess triplets."

"You're wrong, Don. He's gone for good. I came

in here to apologize for putting you in an untenable position. If you don't mind, I'd rather work through my lunch hour."

After closing the connecting door, she headed for her drafting table. Getting back to work was the one panacea that kept the pain at bay.

Forty-five minutes later Jan made an appearance. "I'm going to lunch with Jim now."

Piper got up from her seat and walked over to the desk where she kept her purse. After pulling out a twenty dollar bill, she extended it to her assistant.

"Have lunch on me. It's one of my ways of saying thank you for letting me borrow your ring."

"You don't have to do that." Jan made no move to take it. "I was glad to be of help." After a slight hesitation, "Did it help?"

"I'll never have to worry about his bothering me again."

"You must be the only woman in the world who wouldn't want to be bothered by him."

"Yes, well, you can stop salivating because beneath that gorgeous Spanish physique lurks a Machiavellian brain. He's part Italian you know. Greer didn't trust him the second we went on board the *Piccione* last June. I hate to admit it, but her instincts about that three-tongued Don Juan were right."

"Three-tongued?"

"Yes. He can make love to a woman in French, Spanish and Italian."

"You're kidding!"

"Not at all. To my knowledge he speaks half a dozen romance languages fluently. Among his other, shall we say 'nonsensual' activities, he owns the

Spanish-Portuguese Bank of Iberia, he's a brilliant scholar of Latin and Arabic, and he has written several esoteric books on primogeniture and heraldry.''

''I didn't think a man like him really existed.''

''Yeah, well, he's an original all right.''

''What did he do that made you so furious?''

''He asked me to marry him.''

''You're kidding!'' Jan cried out again. ''You lucky thing…''

''Before you get too excited, let me explain he's in love with a woman who doesn't love him. I think it's a lie. I bet it's a titled woman who can't get out of her marriage.

''Anyway, he needs to find another woman quick so he won't have to marry the sister of his dead fiancée. He just emerged from a year's official mourning.''

''You mean people actually do things like that anymore?''

''Apparently the Pastrana family does. Now Don Juan is on the loose again. Since he had to come to New York on business, he picked on the last Duchess triplet to help him out of his latest scrape. Oh—and get this—'' Piper let out an angry laugh. ''He said it could be dangerous!''

''Maybe you shouldn't laugh. What if the sister of his dead fiancée is the jealous type? Remember when Jim and I went to see *Carmen* at the Metropolitan Opera last month? She was a scary, fiery woman. Maybe this sister is so possessive, she'll try to scratch your eyes out. What's her name?''

''Camilla.''

''It doesn't sound good.''

"Yeah, well, like I said, he won't darken our doorstep again so none of it matters. Go enjoy your lunch!"

"Thanks. Can I bring you something to eat?"

"No, thanks. I'm not hungry."

She expected Jan to leave, but she still hovered. "What's the matter?" The subject of Don Juan was officially closed.

"Could I have my ring back? I'm afraid for Jim to see me without it."

Piper felt the blood drain out of her face.

Slowly she staggered to her feet. "I—I don't have it." Jan looked stunned. "*Nic* does. What did he say to you on his way out?"

"He thanked me for my help and left."

"Did he say where he was going?"

"No."

Oh no. "Jan—"

Her assistant studied her for a moment. "I guess he didn't like being turned down."

"I'll get your ring for you. I swear it," Piper said through gritted teeth. She grabbed her purse. "Before you leave for lunch, will you tell Don I've gone home for a bite to eat? When I get back to the office I'll have your ring with me."

Piper stormed out into the freezing cold to start up the car.

But of course, Nic had said when she'd told him to return Jan's ring. Machiavellian tendencies didn't begin to cover his list of sins.

Nic parked in front of the house where Piper lived in the basement apartment. He had no idea how long his wait would be. A devilish smile broke the corner of his mouth. It all depended on when Jan asked for her ring back.

Suddenly he spotted the car Piper was driving in the rearview mirror of his rental car. Good. He'd wanted to get her away from the office before delivering the *coup de grace*.

She pulled directly behind him and got out. Through the side-view mirror he watched her start toward him.

Like his cousins who'd lived around dark-haired, dark-eyed Mediterranean women all their lives, he too had been captivated by the golden radiance of the Duchess triplets. He loved the way her hair swished around her flushed face like fine gold mesh. Even without the sun shining, it had a brilliance that drew his gaze.

He loved this particular triplet with her slender curves and jewel-like eyes. The first time he'd looked into them, he'd compared them to the shimmering blue-green waters of the Cinque Terre coastline where he and his cousins enjoyed sailing.

Since last June when she'd appeared on the *Piccione,* he'd only been able to look, not touch. It had taken every ounce of self-control to tamp down the ache that had leaped to life deep inside him.

Now that he'd flung the mourning band away, he felt reckless and so consumed with the need to hold and love her, he was trembling with that desire.

The object of his thoughts approached and knocked on the driver's window without hesitation. He pressed the button to lower it.

A faint flowery fragrance from her skin and hair wafted past him. Much like an ember that unexpectedly bursts into flame, her scent ignited every primitive male yearning.

The voluptuous mouth he longed to devour was taut with anger, yet was no less beautiful to him.

"You had no right to drive away with Jan's ring."

"I agree. That's why I gave it to your business partner to return to her. I told him to wait until you'd left the office."

Her eyes set off a flash of incandescent color that rivaled the Northern Lights.

Ready for her next move which was to either return to her car or lock herself in her apartment, Nic levered himself out of the driver's seat and caught up to her. Sheer need drove him to grasp her shoulders and pull her back against his chest.

The only other time he'd had this much physical contact with her was one evening last June when he and his cousins had kidnapped the girls during their attempt to escape on bikes.

Piper had been forced to sit on Nic's lap in the back seat of a car. With the girls' bikes on top of the car, the six of them piled inside for the half hour drive from the countryside beyond Genoa to the harbor.

Thirty minutes of ecstasy to feel her softly rounded warmth against his body. A lifetime of agony because he hadn't been able to do anything about his needs.

Right now she was holding herself rigid, but he could feel her trembling. Because it was freezing out, he had no way of knowing if there wasn't another reason for her condition.

"Please let go of me. People are watching us."

"Let them. There's a lot more I have to say to you, but we need the kind of privacy your office couldn't afford us. You have two choices. Either we talk in your apartment, or my suite at the Kingston Hotel.''

''Not the hotel—'' she fired.

''Very well. Let's go inside your place then.'' Her instinct for survival demanded she face him on her own turf. Since he'd always wanted to see where she lived, Nic couldn't be more pleased.

After relishing the feel of her upper arms for one more moment, he removed his hands so he could follow her to the side steps leading down to her apartment.

She undid the lock. ''I only have a few minutes before I have to get back for an important meeting with Don.''

''It's been canceled. I already explained to him you wouldn't be coming back today.''

Before she could slam the door in his face, he made a quick move inside the warm, inviting living room. Almost at once he came to a standstill in front of a large oil painting which could only be Piper's parents in their latter years.

A long time ago he'd stashed the samples of her calendars in his library at Marbella. When he found himself wanting her too intensely, he would take them out of the drawer and examine her fabulous artwork to feel closer to her.

Yet looking at the painting on the wall, he realized she was a superb portrait painter too. It was a revelation to study the attractive faces and bodies of the two people responsible for bringing the Duchess triplets into the world.

He cleared his throat. ''Odd how some couples in

love grow to look like each other over the years. I can see many of their traits in you.''

She stood next to the coffee table with her arms folded like an adorable schoolteacher waiting for her kindergarten class to come to order.

''It's déjà vu being pursued by one of the Varano cousins again. You've got me trapped, so let's have it. Why have you really come, and what do you really want? Up until now it's all been a bunch of gobbledygook.''

He couldn't help smiling as he turned to face her. ''Gobbledygook?''

''Don't tell me one of Europe's most renowned etymologists hasn't heard that expression before.''

''I can't say I have, but you're right. I've been dancing around you until I could get you where I wanted you.''

Actually she wasn't exactly where he wanted her yet, but being alone with her in this apartment constituted a major miracle and would do for starters.

''Certain information about the jewelry theft gleaned in New York has unearthed a startling new discovery.''

''And?'' she prompted in a bored tone of voice. He could almost hear her tapping her foot, waiting for this to be over so she could boot him out the door. He had news for her…

''It turns out the accident that killed my fiancée in Cortina was no accident. I have every reason to believe the killer wanted both of us dead, but because of a quirk of fate that afternoon, Luc happened to be the one on that tram instead of me.''

CHAPTER THREE

PIPER had been trying hard not to look at him for fear he'd see the hunger in her eyes. But what she'd just heard caused her averted head to lift so they were staring at each other.

"Nina was murdered?" she whispered incredulously.

"She, along with several other innocent victims," came the grim response.

Without being aware of it, Piper's hand went to her throat. "How did you find out?"

"The surveillance cameras trained on the area where Christie's receives merchandise caught a picture of the courier who delivered the jeweled comb. As soon as the CIA agents ran it through a routine check in the international database, one of the Interpol agents tracking an art crime ring recognized him.

"He's a dark-blond Dane in his mid-twenties who uses several aliases. One of the names he goes by is Lars. This is the man."

Piper studied the half dozen copies of photographs Nic took from his pocket. The blond, fit-looking Scandinavian type reminded her of men who spent their time in a gym working out.

"A few months ago some Monet paintings were taken from a private collection in Giverny, France, during a daring armed robbery that left two people dead. This Lars turned out to be one of the hit men

43

they caught on tape. Though the police captured two individuals, he managed to escape and has been on the loose ever since.''

''That's horrible,'' she muttered.

''I faxed my cousins the pictures to apprise them of the new development in the case. The second Luc saw the man, he positively identified him as the person he saw Nina kissing so passionately the day she was killed.''

Piper tore her eyes from the pictures to stare at him in disbelief. ''Your fiancée was unfaithful to you with an armed murderer?''

Nic took the pictures back and put them in his pocket. ''It appears that way, though I had no knowledge of it at the time. My purpose for taking Nina skiing that weekend was to tell her I wanted to end our engagement.''

Shock upon shock.

''End it? I don't understand. I thought your engagement was binding.''

''It should have been, but as the time grew closer to our wedding, I realized I couldn't go through with it.''

With every utterance that came out of his mouth, Piper's mind reeled a little more. ''If you felt that way, why did you get engaged in the first place?''

''From the time I was little, our families were close. At thirty-three I still hadn't found my soul mate, and she was an attractive, eligible woman. Knowing how my father and Señor Robles desired an alliance of our two families, I bowed to the pressure and became engaged to her. I reasoned that at least there would be no surprises in our marriage.

"Unfortunately as the time grew closer to the wedding, I realized I'd only been lying to myself. A union without passion wasn't to be considered. With my mind made up, I decided to plan a ski trip to Cortina where I could break our engagement and we would talk things out.

"After a few ski runs, we left Max and Luc on the slopes, and went back to the chalet where I finally expressed my feelings. I expected tears and anguish from her. Instead she said she needed to be alone to think, then she rushed out of the chalet.

"That's when Luc saw her join up with the other man. He followed them and witnessed their embrace. After they parted, she got in line for the tram. Instead of waiting for Max, who'd gone in the ski shop for a minute, Luc followed her to confront her.

"An hour later Max reached me on his cell phone to tell me there'd been a horrendous tram accident involving a group of skiers, among them Nina and Luc."

Incredible. All of it. "I—I don't know what to say. It's ghastly."

"You're right. Naturally I suffered over her death the way I would have done for any close friend, but I was never in love with her. In light of what I learned in New York this trip, Luc's positive identification of the man named Lars has shed a whole new light on the accident."

"Of course it would." Piper felt chilled and rubbed her hands along her arms to keep the circulation going.

"More than ever it makes sense why the police never could prove the tram suffered a mechanical failure. After talking it over with Luc and Max, we believe Nina may even have played a role in the theft.''

''You're kidding—'' Once again something he'd said had stunned her. There was too much to absorb.

''Not at all. The Robles family visited the Colorno palace long before Nina and I became officially engaged. I remember how interested she was in the collection, but at the time I didn't attach any particular importance to it.

''If she was involved, then I'm assuming she got nervous about her complicity. Maybe she and her lover quarreled. He might have decided to kill her before we got married so she couldn't expose him. For that matter he could have hoped to do away with me at the same time.''

Piper moaned so loud Nic couldn't have helped but hear her.

''Since the ski trip had been on the agenda several weeks in advance, he had time to plan our deaths. But at the last minute the situation took a turn no one expected, and Luc almost lost his leg.''

Visions of her newest brother-in-law leaning on his cane assailed Piper. Thank heaven he'd finally recovered and could live a normal life again. Now he was married to her sister and going to be a father. The possibility that Nic or his cousins could have been killed was so awful, she was still having trouble comprehending it.

''What if Nina was innocent?''

A shadow crossed over his handsome face. ''If she didn't help him to steal the collection and didn't know she was in love with a criminal, then it's an even worse tragedy. Especially since after talking with my cousins we're wondering if Nina's father didn't use his daughter's death to force me into an eventual marriage with Camilla."

A gasp escaped Piper's throat. "You don't really believe that, do you?"

He eyed her soberly. "It's no news that Señor Robles has always felt a certain envy of my father despite their longstanding friendship. I'm the family historian. If you read the histories between our two families going back hundreds of years, you would discover that stranger and more diabolical things have happened."

"Shades of Machiavelli," she whispered.

"Exactly. Señor Robles has a strong dose of it. Otherwise in my father's hearing he wouldn't have suggested a formal mourning period. It was an obvious tactic to keep me from straying until I'm free to wed his other daughter."

"That's archaic!"

"What better way for Señor Robles to become legally aligned with the House of Parma-Bourbon than through Camilla's marriage to me?"

Piper had been pacing the floor, but she stopped. "Luc was right to tell you what he saw. A part of you must be relieved to know Nina had been involved with another man."

"You can't imagine," Nic murmured sounding far away. "It blotted out the guilt I'd been feeling. After all, I'd invited her on that ski trip in the first place. At the time of her death my remorse was so great, it's the only reason I agreed to go into official mourning."

Despite the pain Nic had inflicted on Piper by spurning her, she felt a grudging respect for the way he'd honored his commitment to the woman he couldn't bring himself to marry. "If Luc hadn't said anything, then—"

"Then I would still be struggling with that destructive emotion," he broke in. "After Luc told Max about Nina's lover, they felt it vital I hear the truth so neither Señor Robles or my father could manipulate me further."

"Does your father expect you to marry Camilla?"

"Probably, but he's still grieving over Nina whom he loved like a daughter. That's why it's my intention to return to Marbella with a bona fide wife.

"Not only will it put an end to any expectations my father might have, it will send the unmistakable message to the Robles family that I consider my moral obligation to them officially over. However to keep the peace between the two families, I intend to maintain a close relationship with them."

He cocked his head. "That's where you would come in if you were to agree to be my bride. As Luc and Max pointed out, you're the perfect person to carry it off."

Her heart plunged to her feet. "So this was *their* idea."

"It's a good one. The Robles family will be forced to treat you with deference. After your convincing performance with Don a little while ago, I have no doubts you'll play your part brilliantly. I realize you haven't met Camilla yet, but don't worry. You'll be more than a match for her. She has a fiery nature too."

"Too?" Piper's eyes flashed blue-green sparks. "Is that supposed to be a compliment or a condemnation?"

His gaze wandered over her features with slow deliberation. "Definitely a compliment. Because Camilla's pride will be hurt, she'll try to find a weakness in you, but she won't be successful because she'll be tangling wi—"

"With the last notorious Duchess triplet," Piper finished for him in a withering tone.

"As my wife," he went on speaking, "you'll play hostess for many business and social gatherings which will include the Robles family. Using your warmth and charm, you'll attempt to be Camilla's friend.

"It would be natural for you to turn to her for friendship. Ask her to help you with the kinds of things women love to do, like shopping at the best boutiques."

"I *hate* to shop—" Piper blurted. "It takes too much time from my painting. I only go to the store for something when I have to!"

One dark brow quirked. "That's the artist in you, like Michelangelo who never wanted to come down from the scaffolding while he was painting the Sistine Chapel."

She bristled. "I wouldn't go quite that far."

"That's good to hear." His teasing tone made her blood bubble. "The more you mix with Camilla and her friends and observe what goes on in the Robles household, the better.

"I want you to win her around as if you had no idea her father had expected her to be the next Pastrana fiancée. If Camilla has any information about her sister's secret love life, you can be my eyes and ears.

"I'm counting on her confiding in you that she

knew about Lars and where he lives, where the two lovers used to meet. Camilla will relish telling you things like that to injure you and hurt me for thwarting her. You might pick up on something that will help us determine whether Nina was involved in the theft or not.''

At this point Jan's comment that Camilla might be jealous enough to do bodily harm didn't sound so far off the mark. ''In other words you want a wife who'll spy for you.''

''That's right. Perhaps there won't be anything incriminating to learn. Whatever happens, my role will be vastly easier to carry out if I return home with an American wife who is anxious to fit in socially.''

''What role is that?'' Piper demanded.

''While there's a manhunt on for the killer, my cousins and I are going to concentrate our free time on helping with the investigation.''

''That's the job of the police!''

His features tightened. ''After what happened to Luc, and for the sake of our family, we have a vested interest in capturing this particular criminal and the person he takes orders from.''

''So you don't think he's working alone?''

''No. Someone else has to be the mastermind. Lars is one of several who carry out the dirty work.''

Piper shivered at his ferocity. ''I'm not the right person for the job.''

''I thought a Duchess wasn't afraid of anything.''

Her body stiffened. ''I'm not! But in case it escaped your notice, I don't speak or understand Spanish. Some spy I would make!''

''That's not a problem. I'll teach you as we go.

You'll pick it up fast. Besides, what is it you Americans say? Actions speak louder than words?''

"They also say you can't get blood out of a turnip!"

His deep chuckle was so attractive, it made her nervous. "You're no turnip. I've seen you in action, Señorita Piperre, but I also realize this is no light thing I'm asking of you. That's why I'll make sure you're always safe."

The more he kept talking, the more she could imagine herself falling in with his wishes.

"Once the culprits have been caught, then we'll get our marriage annulled. You can come back to New York and your career. Whatever you want."

Whatever I want? "In that case, why would we have to get married?"

"To be convincing of course," he answered suavely. "You realize we'll have to act the part of newlyweds. If we're truly married, we won't have to pretend anything. It's imperative we don't allow anyone to know what's really going on, not even your sisters."

After the stand Piper had made never to forgive Nic or set foot on European soil, her sisters would accuse her of caving, and she wouldn't be able to tell them why. Not until the whole farce was over.

"Everyone, particularly the Robles family, will have to believe we've been in love for a long time and eloped because we couldn't wait for a formal engagement and wedding."

Any second now her heart was going to bound out of her body because the pain was too great. Her mouth had gone dry. "If I say no, who's your second choice for a wife?"

"Consuela Munoz, the editor working with me on my latest book."

The name came so swiftly to his tongue, Piper's jealousy was instantly aroused. "Is she titled?"

"No, but both families have met her on several occasions and are aware I've spent enough time with her to have established a...relationship."

Pain, pain, pain.

Piper stifled her groan. Was this editor the woman he loved but couldn't marry? Or had Piper credited Nic with too much nobility and he'd carried on a private liaison with her over the last year? Twelve months was a long time for a man like him to go without a woman.

Filled with fresh anguish she said, "Tell me something, Nic. What was the point of bringing a baby into the conversation earlier?"

"As far as I'm concerned, I'm willing to make my marriage to you real if you find yourself wishing you had a child like your sisters. Since you don't want money for helping me, a baby's the one thing I could try to give you.

"Naturally if one came along, we'd stay together. It would provide me with an heir, and of course make my parents happy. It's all up to you. Just so you know, when my cousins and I took a vote between you and Consuela, it was unanimous that the feisty Duchess triplet was our first choice."

On that note he moved toward the door. "I'm in room 220 at the Kingsport. You already gave me your answer at the office earlier, but if you should change your mind, call me at the hotel. I'll be leaving for Spain in the morning.''

Long after he'd disappeared, Piper was still confused. In exchange for her help, he'd just offered her a life with him if she wanted it. Everything was there for the taking—marriage, the possibility of a baby.

But not his love.

An hour later when her tears were spent, she phoned Don. But the second she heard his voice, she broke down again.

''Want to talk about it?''

''Oh Don— I don't know what to do.'' The thought of Nic asking his editor to marry him was killing her. How long had *that* association been going on?

Piper knew he'd authored several nonfiction books. Maybe his editor was only pretending she didn't love him because she knew he was in mourning.

What if all this time she'd been waiting until he no longer wore the black arm band before she let him know how she felt? If that was the case...

''Piper?''

''Yes?'' she answered in an emotional voice.

''Something tells me I'm about to lose a partner.''

February 1
Kingston, New York

''Piper Duchess de Pastrana—you have no idea how pleased I am to see you married at last. Women weren't meant to be on their own.''

Mr. Carlson, the Duchess family attorney, held both her hands while he bestowed his beaming, patriarchal smile on her.

Greer and Olivia would have broken down in fits of laughter to see the way he was looking at her. "May I be the first to congratulate you and your husband on the beginning of your new life together."

Piper smiled back at him, hoping she could contain herself long enough to get out of there before she really lost it. "Thank you for letting us have the ceremony in your office, Mr. Carlson. It was kind of your friend from the county clerk's office to marry us."

"We're very grateful," Nic concurred. Since the passionate kiss he'd bestowed on her mouth at the end of the ceremony, he'd kept a possessive hold around her waist.

In fact he'd put a lot of energy into their first kiss in order to fool everyone, but it hadn't fooled Piper for a second. Which was why she hadn't allowed it to go on and on, in case he got any funny ideas that she was enjoying it.

In agreeing to marry him and stay married until the killer was caught, she'd told him point-blank she had no intentions of sleeping with him. So if he couldn't handle it, then he was welcome to make his editor the sacrificial cow, to which he'd remained silent on the subject.

"Later on we'll be having a church wedding in Marbella for the whole family to attend," she heard Nic confide to the attorney. *Oh no we won't.* "But we couldn't wait that long to say our vows."

Mr. Carlson's smile couldn't be any wider. His gaze fell on the plain gold wedding band adorning her ring finger. It wasn't the wedding she'd dreamed of all her life, so she'd refused to let him give her anything else.

"I'm honored that you would turn to me, Piper. I

have no doubts your parents were looking on, my dear. How delighted they must be to know that all three of their precious pigeons have flown to new homes to roost and rear families.''

Piper's father had always called his daughters his precious pigeons after the beautiful white Duchesse pigeon which the Italians had named in honor of the Duchess of Parma. She almost choked in hysteria over Mr. Carlson's words, but somehow she managed to control herself. ''I'm sure they are.''

''Your parents must have been inspired to create the Husband Fund. You can't imagine how gratified I am that those checks I handed to you the day you girls assembled to hear your father's will, led you to meet the Varano cousins.''

''It was our lucky day,'' Nic commented.

The older man smiled at her new husband who looked splendid in a formal silk suit of slate blue. Piper had dressed in the white chiffon she'd worn at the Falcon villa the night before the Grand Prix. She'd insisted she would use whatever she had on hand for the quickie wedding.

''As I told Greer when she called me from the Genoa airport last year, a woman needs a man to make her world complete.''

Nic was loving it. He nodded his proud head in agreement even though he knew that call had been a plea for help so the girls could get away from him and his cousins.

But you'd never convince Mr. Carlson of that fact now.

While Piper was still smiling beatifically at her

father's good friend and attorney, one of Greer's slogans printed on their calendars popped into her head.

Unable to resist needling Nic she said, ''As I told Nic when I agreed to marry him, 'If you need to get it done, ask a woman.'''

Mr. Carlson might not get the thrust of her words, but Nic understood. She didn't want him forgetting the reason why she'd put her career on temporary hold while Don ran their business in the interim.

Nic needed a prop to hold him up while he cracked the murder case wide-open. What he didn't know was that in the end, fear had prompted her to agree to his marriage proposal. Fear because Nic and his cousins were the killer's targets.

Luc had almost died in the accident. If Nic had decided to go after Nina that day to make sure she was all right, he might not have lived to tell about it.

What if the killer decided that any of the Varano men were fair game because he suspected they were on to him? That meant Piper's sisters could be in danger too. Piper was prepared to do anything to help the people she loved, even if it meant befriending Camilla to track down this Lars.

The thought of life without the Varanos—without Nic—

Piper couldn't fathom it. Not now.

After phoning Nic at his hotel the other night with her answer, she'd worked him hard over the next three days. She had to admit that with him pitching in, the packing got done in record time.

Her furnishings had been placed aboard the Pastrana jet. The apartment was spotless. Nic even managed to get $700.00 out of a used car dealer for her dad's old car.

One close call happened when he'd found a mockup of her newest calendar not meant for curious eyes. It had fallen behind the bed. Luckily she'd grabbed it from him before he'd been able to look inside, thus avoiding catastrophe.

There'd also been an amusing moment when he'd discovered Olivia's rock polishing machine and had commandeered it for himself to take back to Marbella.

"You never know when this might come in handy," he'd muttered before boxing it for the men he'd hired to carry out to the truck. By the mysterious look on his face Piper had an idea Nic knew exactly what he was going to do with it.

That playful side of him, so rarely in evidence, broke through every barrier to make her fall more deeply in love with him.

The most emotional moment came when she asked him to carry two 36 x 60 inch oil paintings from the basement storage room to the living room for the movers to carefully pack.

Nic took so long, she left the bathroom where she'd been scouring the tile floor to find out what was wrong. When she entered the storage room, she discovered him standing before them deep in thought. She took his utter stillness as a compliment of sorts.

The paintings were her wedding gifts to her sisters. She'd been waiting until they came to New York so they could decide on the right frames.

The one of Greer showed Max bending over her on the *Piccione* right before the three girls dove overboard to escape. Piper would never forget the hungry look in Max's eyes, or the way Greer gazed up at him, her gorgeous lavender eyes burning with love for him.

Piper had caught their private look on canvas. If ever two people were on fire for each other...

In the other painting, she'd captured a magical moment between Luc and Olivia outside the Pastrana private chapel before their wedding when they didn't know they were being observed.

As Olivia stared up into Luc's love smitten face, her eyes glowed a blue so hot and dazzling, the artist in Piper had mentally recorded that look of passion between them and reproduced it on canvas at a later date.

"The packers are waiting to crate these, Nic."

He didn't move a muscle of his tall, hard-muscled physique.

"Your paintings are magnificent," came a deep voice she didn't recognize because it sounded so husky. "My cousins will be overcome with emotion."

Piper started to pull the nearest one toward the open doorway. "They'll probably think the canvases are too big and won't know where to hang them." She'd blown off his compliments to hide the tremor in her voice.

Nic intercepted her and carried it to the front room before going back for the other one. From that point on he was the one to oversee the crating before they were transported to the plane. That left Piper to make a last visit upstairs to her landlady.

She gave her the keys and a hug. There was no guarantee that when she returned to New York at a later date, this apartment would be available.

On their way to the airport in Nic's rental car, a

teary eyed Piper looked back at the house across the street where she'd lived for the first twenty-six years of her life. In her mind's eye she could see her family outside on the porch. No five people had ever been happier.

But that period of time was over.

As Dr. Arnavitz had said, her girlhood was behind her now. Her sisters were married women, and she was about to become a wife herself, with one enormous difference—

Nic had married her so she could run interference and spy for him. There wouldn't be a wedding night. When he no longer had any use for her, their marriage would be annulled.

By the time they reached the freeway, Piper made up her mind she would be the best spy on earth and help Nic solve this crime in record time. She'd promised Don she would be back soon, and she'd meant every word. It was a case of self-preservation!

After escorting Piper on board the jet and seeing to her comfort, Nic excused himself on the pretext of talking to his pilot.

Pulling out his cell phone, he punched one of the digits and soon heard a familiar voice on the other end. "*Eh bien, mon vieux,* am I now speaking to a married man?"

Nic bowed his head. "You are. But she's coming kicking and screaming all the way, if you know what I mean."

"As long as she's got your ring on her finger, nothing else matters."

That's what Nic had kept telling himself until he'd

spent a torturous wedding night knowing she was sleeping soundly in the next room. At the moment his mood was foul. "Luc—are you alone?"

"Yes. Where are you now?"

"At the airport. Is everything set?"

"*Absolument.* When you arrive at the villa, the family will be here en masse."

"What pretext did you finally come up with?"

"Max's birthday is next week. We decided it was the best reason to get everyone together. So I suggested to Maman we throw a big party for him tonight because I'll be away at a robotics conference on his birthday.

"I told her you would try to make it back from New York in time for the celebration. Olivia and Greer rushed to help her. They have everything organized. All the parents will be there. No one has any idea Piper will be walking through the door with you."

"Perfect. We're bringing a present for Max guaranteed to knock him senseless."

"*Ah oui?*"

"*Sí.*" Piper had a present for Luc too, one that would rock his foundation the second he saw it.

"Max and I have arranged for extra security. You'll be watched from the moment you land in Nice."

Nic sucked in his breath. "I promised Piper no harm would come to her. I pray to God that's true. If anything happened to her…"

"It won't," Luc came back fiercely. "We won't let anything happen to any of us. By the way, we're not having this party any too soon."

"What's going on?"

"Maman was talking to your mother. She let it slip

that your father is glad the mourning period is now over. He's anxious for his only son to find a new love interest and plans to sit down with you for a fatherly chat as soon as you return from New York.''

Nic's jaw hardened. ''Papa's worries are over. I've already claimed my soul mate. Tonight she'll put on a performance that will fool even her sisters. Piper believes they're in mortal danger and is coming to the rescue. All for one, one for all.''

''It works every time.''

''See you this evening, Luc.''

''A bientôt.''

Nic hung up and walked back to the cabin to strap himself in. His pilot was ready to take off.

The scream of the engines was music to his ears. Nic had counted on Piper's love of adventure to take the bait, even if it spelled danger. So far she hadn't disappointed him.

His new bride was in fighting mode sitting there in the seat next to him, her chin jutting prominently. She was wise to keep her emotional distance from him since his own savage instincts were threatening to take over.

In time they would...

CHAPTER FOUR

THE luxurious black stretch car with the Falcon crest climbed higher and higher until Piper caught sight of Luc's childhood home in Monaco-Ville. Much like the night before the Grand Prix last June, the beautiful nineteenth-century Provençal villa called the *Clos Des Falcons* gave off a welcoming glow.

But tonight there were several differences. She didn't see as many boats in the famous harbor below, and the cool February air reminded her it was still winter.

Of course there was a monumental difference since last summer. All three Duchess sisters were now married to the Varano cousins, and Nic expected her to act like a starry-eyed bride.

That would be impossible since her pain had increased threefold after spending her wedding night alone in the hotel room next to Nic's. The only consolation to make it bearable was the fact that Consuela Munoz wasn't wearing his gold wedding band.

In the next little while, the news that Piper had married him would reach the people inside the villa. It would produce every emotion ranging from joy to shock, surprise, pain, maybe even animosity on the part of Señor de Pastrana, her new father-in-law.

Nic had prepared her well. "Your job, Señora de Pastrana, is to smile a lot and act happy while I do the talking." She supposed she could comply with his wishes to that degree. The trick was to make certain her sisters didn't see through the smile pasted on her face.

Too much euphoria and Greer would sense overkill. Too little and Olivia would suspect all was not as it should be.

Nic had bought her the new ivory colored silk suit with the pearl buttons for a wedding present. He'd been adamant about it. The elegant outfit exuded a bridal image, especially since he'd pinned a corsage to her jacket.

Her hair was longer than it had been last summer. She'd chosen to let it fall loose from a side part.

"Before we go inside, I have another wedding present for you. Give me your hand."

Her head jerked around to the man in the stunning black tuxedo sitting next to her in the back of the limo. He wore a yellow rose in his lapel. Their bodies never touched, but she felt his intoxicating masculine aura as surely as she breathed in the delicious fragrance from the flowers.

With her heart tearing along like the riptide, she extended her right hand.

"Your other hand," he said in a deep velvety voice that stirred her senses.

"I already have a gold band."

"You're a bride of the House of Pastrana and Parma-Bourbon now." He reached across her lap and grasped her left hand. His touch sent a shockwave through her sensitized body.

"This pearl, called the teardrop of the moon, is a family heirloom. I had it reset for you. Only an Anglo-Saxon bride with hair of spun gold should wear it."

The words he'd just spoken rendered her speechless. When she looked down at the large, round, blemish-free white pearl set in gold filigree pushed next to the gold band, her breath caught.

In her witless state he raised her hand to his lips and kissed the palm.

No, Nic—

Trembling from the contact, she pulled her hand away. "I—I can't wear this."

His features closed up. "If you don't, my parents won't be convinced our wedding was real."

"But it's too big a responsibility. What if I lost it?" she cried out in anxiety.

"What if you did?"

"Nic—don't pretend with me. With such a history behind it, this pearl is priceless. I'm terrified at the thought of something happening to it. Have you forgotten the only reason we're together now is because of the stolen Duchesse collection?" Her question rang out in the confines of the limo.

"I've forgotten nothing," came his innocuous response. "Don't look now, but our arrival has been announced, and your sisters have followed my cousins out the front door. Give me your mouth, *mi amor*."

Her surprised gasp was lost as his lips rushed to cover hers. He began kissing her the way she'd always wanted him to kiss her, as if she was the only thing of importance in his universe.

Nic— Her heart wept. It was all for show.

How could he devour her with this kind of raw passion when he was in love with another woman? From the moment she'd said "I do," every one of his actions and gestures, every comment was all part of a role he was playing.

Their marriage was counterfeit. She was the counterfeit Pastrana bride, chosen to prevent a marriage to Camilla from ever taking place. The lustrous pearl ring mocked Piper. Yet she was too entrenched in this dangerous deception to back out now.

She'd agreed to help Nic with the investigation— for him, his family and her beloved sisters. Bodyguards had been assigned to prevent another murder. Piper had a job to infiltrate the Robles family and see if she could learn anything to help the case. The whole situation was surreal and would remain that way until the killer was apprehended.

Someone opened the door on her side of the limo. Before Nic relinquished her mouth, he'd deliberately planned for them to get caught in a hungry kiss that her sisters couldn't possibly misinterpret.

"Piper!"

"I'll let you go for now," he whispered into her hair unexpectedly. Then he released her to the cries of her excited sisters who were pulling her out of the car.

The next few minutes were a blur of happy tears as the three of them jumped up and down hugging. It had been so long since she'd seen them. Too long.

"You're wearing yellow roses!" Olivia blurted.

"Let's see your left hand," Greer demanded. Piper extended it for their perusal. Both sisters gasped at the size and beauty of the pearl. "When did you and Nic get married?"

She swallowed hard. "Yesterday."

"Yesterday was February First," Greer murmured, obviously putting two and two together.

"Where?" Olivia cried.

"In Mr. Carlson's office."

Her lips curved upward. "You've got to be kidding!"

"No. You wouldn't believe how hilarious he was."

For the next few minutes she regaled them with the details until they were howling with laughter over his patriarchal attitude where women were concerned. It provided a wonderful cover for Piper to hide the horrible truth that her husband wasn't in love with her. But as their hilarity subsided, she realized it was time to change the subject.

Studying her sisters whose familiar faces were indescribably dear to her she said, "Neither one of you looks pregnant yet."

Greer's shrewd regard trapped hers. "Neither do you…yet."

Smile, Piper. Smile your mysterious smile so Greer won't figure out something's wrong here.

"At least we know my baby will come in last. The question is, *whose* is going to make an appearance first? Yours or Olivia's?"

Greer continued to stare at her, making Piper more and more uncomfortable. "I didn't think anything Nic could do would ever cause you to forgive him."

"Neither did I," Olivia concurred in a sober tone. "As I recall, you said he was your mortal enemy. Unless you two had assignations behind everyone's back, you must admit your marriage to him on his first day of freedom is a little over the top."

Piper needed to say something to dispel any suspicions that she'd married him for any other reason than love. She didn't want them to know how close all three

Varano cousins had come to being killed in Cortina, let alone that they would be in danger until the man called Lars was arrested.

She looked from one to the other. "I have a confession to make."

"Go ahead," they said at the same time.

"I went to a psychiatrist last August. He helped me sort out my feelings."

Greer frowned. "Since when do the Duchess triplets need a psychiatrist?"

"When there's just one triplet left," she replied in a small voice. "With Dr. Arnavitz's help I realized that I was taking out a big portion of my anger on Nic. In reality I was suffering over losing you guys."

"You didn't lose us!" Olivia scoffed.

"Yes I did. It was horrible. When I finally figured out where a lot of my pain was coming from, I could see that I'd been punishing Nic for rejecting me. But the punishment didn't fit the crime.

"The only reason he rejected me was because he'd made a commitment to go into mourning and was determined to honor it. When I was able to be rational about it, I realized he's a noble man. That's a quality I always admired in Daddy."

At the mention of their father, all their eyes dimmed for a moment.

"Dr. Arnavitz told me to practice patience. He said that if the feelings between Nic and me were real, then Nic would do something about it after his mourning period was over."

It was scary how easily the lies came to her lips, but Piper was prevaricating for the best of reasons.

"So I took his advice and got busy working on

some other projects. You can see what happened. Nic flew to New York the other day to see me." She paused for effect. "I— It's what I'd been praying for."

Piper said the last in a hushed tone so the men standing on the other side of the car couldn't hear her and figure out she really was in love with Nic.

Whatever else might not ring true to her sisters, the wobble in her voice was a hundred percent genuine. That little sound seemed to satisfy their questions for the time being because they each looped an arm through hers before they moved inside the villa.

Greer brought them to a halt in the center of the elegant foyer Piper had stood in before. "The families are in the drawing room. You do realize this news is going to send Nic's father into shock."

She nodded.

"Thank goodness the Robles family wasn't invited to this party," Olivia whispered.

"After we leave for Marbella, Nic has asked me to befriend Camilla and her family."

Both sisters raised their eyebrows. "Good luck."

Suddenly Piper felt herself propelled away from her sisters into Max's strong arms. "Welcome to the family, *bellissima*. You've not only made our cousin deliriously happy, you've saved two marriages."

"Max is right," Luc chimed in before claiming her for himself and kissing her on both cheeks. "With you back on our turf, maybe our wives will finally settle down and pay attention to *us* for a change."

Piper flashed him a mischievous smile. "My sisters must have paid *some* attention to you. You're both expecting babies after all," she quipped to hide her agony.

In a heartbeat a pair of masculine hands slid to her shoulders from behind, kneading them with growing insistence. "I'm anxious to receive that same kind of attention from you later." Nic had murmured the words loud enough against her hot cheek for the others to hear. "Shall we go in the drawing room and get Max's birthday party started?"

"I'll do the honors." Luc put an arm around his wife and opened the tall French doors leading into the other room. Max and Greer followed. Nic ushered Piper along behind them while she braced herself for the ordeal ahead.

From the foyer she glimpsed three sets of beautifully dressed parents, plus Max's sister and her husband seated in the lavishly appointed room. They were conversing and enjoying cocktails. The only person missing was Cesar, Luc's brother, who Nic had told her was practicing to compete in the British Grand Prix.

"Attention everyone." At the sound of Luc's voice, all eyes swerved toward him. "Nic made it in time for the celebration, but he didn't come alone. He picked up a bride on his trip to New York."

The palpable silence that followed his unexpected announcement didn't bother Piper nearly as much as the look of shock on the face of Señor de Pastrana. His patrician features seemed to harden to granite. Pain—surprise—anger—so many emotions glinted from his dark eyes. It was an unsettling moment Piper would remember all her life.

Nic's Italian mother was first up from the love seat. She swept across the room to embrace Piper. The others followed suit.

"Niccolo has given us a daughter-in-law at last. I can't believe it. Welcome to the family."

Her warm brown eyes displayed real affection, making Piper feel a total fraud. But when she remembered why she'd agreed to marry Nic, and what was at stake, she was able to pull herself together.

"I've loved your son for a very long time, Señora de Pastrana."

"Call me Maria."

Nic put his arm around Piper's shoulders. His male warmth dissolved her bones. "I lost my heart to her on the *Piccione*, Mama."

"I can see that, otherwise she wouldn't be wearing the family pearl. Has Nic told you the story behind it?"

Piper blinked. "I only know it's an heirloom and I'm terrified of losing it."

Her comment caused everyone crowded around them to chuckle. Soon Piper was besieged with a genuine outpouring of affection. Except from Nic's father who had yet to welcome her into the family.

Closer now Piper detected a dull red flush on his face. Her appearance wearing Nic's ring had dashed the older man's dreams for his only son. Piper had it in her heart to feel sorry for him.

As Nic had told her, Nina had been like a daughter to him. He'd loved her. To see her supplanted by someone else, no matter who it was, couldn't help but sting.

"Congratulations, Señora de Pastrana." He gave her a stiff nod, but obviously couldn't bring himself to kiss her.

Under the circumstances Piper wouldn't have expected anything more from him. After a lifetime of wanting something else, wanting someone else for Nic, it wouldn't have been honest of him to give her a fatherly embrace.

"Thank you, *Señor*." A lump lodged in her throat. "You have such a wonderful son. I'm going to do everything in my power to make him happy."

Nic had already put a possessive arm around her hip. He pulled her against his side in an intimate gesture. "When Piper agreed to marry me, she made me happier than I've ever been in my life, Papa."

Piper's new husband was a master actor. She could tell everyone who wasn't in on the scheme had bought his lie.

"When did your nuptials take place?" his father asked in a clipped tone.

"Yesterday."

The two men eyed each other like old warriors. Lines bracketed the older man's mouth, giving him a gaunt appearance. A weight descended on Piper's heart to see his struggle.

He might be an autocratic man who, because he'd been born a royal, had certain expectations for his handsome, brilliant son. But he loved Nic, and this was the new millennium, not the thirteenth century when marriages were made to join two royal houses in order to aggrandize their power and property.

"I couldn't wait any longer to marry her, so we arranged for a ceremony in the law office of Mr. Carlson, a close friend of Piper's father. But now that we're home, we'll plan a ceremony with the priest in the estate chapel for the whole family to witness."

Nic's hand bit into her waist just enough to warn her not to protest.

"We'll give a party right away announcing your marriage," his mother exclaimed with a light in her eyes that looked heartfelt to Piper.

"That would be wonderful," she spoke up. "I'll do everything I can to help."

"We'll all help." This from Luc's mother.

"No festivities will take place until you've met with Benito and Ynes."

"I plan to take care of that tomorrow evening after Piper and I have flown to Marbella, Papa."

"How exciting to have another Duchess join the family!" Nic's mother exclaimed to dispel the tension. "It's extraordinary to think our sons married triplets!"

Max's mother nodded. "Surely there must be a scientific explanation for such a phenomenon."

Olivia nodded. "When we were younger, we read everything we could about triplets and twins. We learned it's not unusual to be attracted to the same people. Something in the genes."

"Scientific or not, the first sight of the Duchesses of Kingston took our collective breath," Nic asserted, almost crushing Piper against him. "I know I've never been the same since." His cousins seconded Nic's remark.

While Piper was still staring up at him in astonishment because just then he'd sounded like he'd meant it, he lowered his mouth and kissed her in front of everyone.

He kept it within the bounds of decency, but barely. Piper weaved in place and had to clutch him for support.

The family applauded.

When he finally lifted his head he said, "As long as we've crashed Max's birthday party, we might as well give him his present now. Everyone wait here. I'll be right back."

He brushed her lips again before disappearing from the drawing room. So far his portrayal of the besotted bridegroom had gone without a flaw. Piper staggered to the nearest couch.

Her sisters joined her while the rest of the family went back to their places to finish their drinks. In a few seconds Nic reappeared with one of the huge canvases. He turned it around.

Piper heard Max murmur something indistinct. He grabbed his wife's hand and the two of them walked up to the painting.

"Piper—" her sister exclaimed with so much emotion, it didn't even sound like Greer.

Max wheeled around and stared at her. His black eyes looked suspiciously bright. "You're a genius. We'll treasure this forever."

"I too am in awe of my wife's talent," Nic announced. "There's more!"

Leaving Max to keep the gift upright, he went out to the foyer. Pretty soon he came back in with another canvas identical in size.

"Your birthday won't be for a few more months, Luc, but Piper and I wanted you to have this now."

When Nic displayed the painting for everyone to see, more gratifying cries of astonishment resounded in the drawing room.

By now Olivia wept openly in Luc's arms. He turned to Piper. From the distance separating them he said, "You *are* a genius." His voice was as husky as Max's had been. "Thank you, *chérie*."

"You're welcome."

More conversation ensued as everyone gathered round to examine Piper's artwork.

She got up from the couch and moved closer. "I thought I'd let you decide on the frames since I didn't know where you would want to hang them."

Max smiled at his wife. "I know exactly where ours is going."

"So do I," Luc murmured before kissing Olivia.

"I'm feeling a little left out," Nic said to no one in particular.

Both Piper's sisters hurried over to give him hugs. "You mean you haven't seen the calendar Piper created of you?" Greer questioned.

"You're the feature of the month on every page!" Olivia declared.

"Am I another kind of pigeon?"

"No—they're real life drawings of you. I told her it was her best work!"

Piper felt his intense regard. "I must have missed it while we were packing."

Praying her face hadn't gone blood-red she said, "When we all came home from Europe to get ready for Greer's wedding, I did several mockups featuring the Varano cousins for a line of men's calendars."

He darted her a sly grin. "Playboys of the Riviera?"

Heat swept through her body. "No. The Husband Fund Trio."

"The Husband Fund Trio? How very appropriate," Nic murmured with a distinctly pleased smile.

"Before you get too excited, you need to know Don didn't think they'd go over the same way as my pigeon drawings. To be honest, I'd forgotten about them. He's probably tossed them by now."

"I doubt he would get rid of anything you created. I'll give him a call and ask him to courier them to me."

"Trust me. He threw them out. He didn't want his friends to see them."

Piper had her own copies, but they were safely stored in a box she'd already packed safely out of Nic's sight.

"You mean Huey didn't want Louey and Dewey's feelings to get hurt?"

Those were the names of some famous ducks in an American comic strip the girls had nicknamed their former boyfriends, and Nic had picked up on it.

"Our win, their loss," he muttered, flashing what Greer always called that good-old-boy-network smile at his cousins. They smiled back exactly the same way.

Piper didn't dare look at her sisters just then. It was perfect timing when Luc's mother chose that moment to tell them dinner was ready. Everyone filed into the dining room.

Piper tried not to look at Nic's father while they ate. Though Max kept the entertainment alive opening his gifts, she was glad when the meal came to a close.

To her relief Luc announced that the cousins and their wives were moving on to his villa for the night. Goodnights were said, but in the swirl of activity, all Piper noticed was Señor de Pastrana's curt nod in their direction before Nic ushered her out to the limo.

Once inside, he pulled her onto his lap and kissed

the nape of her neck during the short drive to the villa located above Monaco-Ville. The touch of his lips against her hot skin reduced her to a quivery lump. After they arrived in the courtyard, she could hardly walk once he'd helped her out of the car.

Olivia had sent Piper photos of their home, so she knew what it looked like inside and out. But no picture ever did justice to the real thing. The beautiful two-story pink villa with the blue shutters screamed at Piper to get it down on canvas.

But it needed a hot July sun for the full effect. A pain pierced her heart to realize that by the time summer came, she would have fulfilled her purpose for coming to Europe, and would be back in Kingston again. Alone...

While the men assembled in Luc's study, Olivia took her and Greer upstairs to show them what bedrooms they would be sleeping in. The one for Piper and Nic was at the end of the corridor. Their luggage had already been brought up.

The second Piper saw the queen-size bed, she panicked and rushed over to one of the windows. "What a magnificent view!"

"I never tire of looking at it." A strange silence followed Olivia's comment while she stared at Piper. "After the pain you've lived through since last year, who would have ever dreamed you'd be sleeping in this room with Nic tonight."

Piper needed to guide the conversation in another direction before Olivia made any more personal observations or started asking questions. Like how come she and Nic got married so fast when only a week ago she'd still refused to acknowledge his existence?

''The pain is behind me and I don't want to talk about it. Did I tell you Mrs. Weyland sends her love to you guys? She says that whenever you get homesick for Kingston, you're welcome to stay at her house. It's an open invitation.''

''When our adoption goes through and the baby is old enough to travel, Max and I will fly to New York and pay her a visit. As long as we're on the subject, does Tom know you got married?''

She nodded to Greer. ''Don told him. All the guys are dating other people now, so we're off the hook. With Jan managing the office, I don't feel bad about him running things from there. I plan to do work for him from Nic's villa. He says there's enough room in his library for a drafting table.''

Greer's brows lifted. ''Now that you're Señora de Pastrana, are you going to have that kind of time?''

Actually Piper would have plenty of time while Nic and her brothers-in-law were out pursuing the killer. In fact they were downstairs right now going over their plans. Just thinking about the danger they were in sent a shudder through her body.

''I'll draw in the evenings while Nic's working on his latest book. During the day I'm going to take Spanish lessons and thought I'd ask Camilla Robles to be my teacher.''

Olivia shook her head. ''You can't do that.''

''Olivia's right,'' Greer declared. ''When she learns you stole Nic from her, I'm afraid there'll be war between the two families.''

''Nic's aware of that. He asked me to befriend her because he doesn't want to make enemies. I think it's the perfect way to win her friendship. Both of you have been taking lessons to learn how to speak Italian and French. I'll do the same thing."

The idea had just come to her, but when Piper thought about it, she realized it would be a means of invading the Robles household and seeing the other woman on a fairly constant basis.

"Except that my teacher doesn't want to wipe up the floor with me," Greer drawled. "I've only been around Camilla a few times, but I've noticed she has a short fuse."

Nic had told Piper virtually the same thing. "Since he asked me this favor, I have to try."

"Then watch your back. Luc says she's been secretly in love with him for years."

At Olivia's warning, Piper felt like someone had just walked over her grave. Neither of her sisters knew the theft had turned into a murder case, or that Nic expected Piper's help in solving it.

"It's important to Nic he maintain a good relationship with the Robles family. Somehow there has to be a way to soften her up."

"I'm not sure that's possible," Greer muttered. "Nic has been a big part of the Robles sisters' lives for years."

Except that neither Robles sister knew Nic had always loved someone else. Piper could hardly bear it.

"I know, so I've got to work extra hard to smooth things out."

"Mom was right about you," Olivia commented. "You've always been the peacemaker."

Greer put a hand on Piper's arm. "Nic's luckier than he knows."

"But I do know," his deep, vibrant voice broke in on her sisters' conversation.

Giving her a hug, Greer said, "I think your husband wants you to himself, so we'll say goodnight."

Olivia rushed to hug her too. "If you need anything, just let me know. Tomorrow we'll have breakfast together before you fly to Marbella."

They both hugged Nic before leaving the bedroom. After they shut the door, Piper's heart thundered like a kettledrum to find herself alone with him.

"Your performance tonight was so convincing, Father didn't walk out on the celebration."

She bit her lip. "Did you expect him to?"

"Yes."

A tremor rocked her body. "Why didn't you tell me that before now?"

After a palpable silence, "I took a calculated risk. Father doesn't want to like you, but he can't ignore the fact that you were noble enough to absent yourself completely from my life until the mourning period was over.

"Furthermore, your paintings thrilled everyone including my father who admires a true artistic gift. Your work reveals you're a woman of surprising depth and substance. I saw the recognition of those qualities ignite his eyes and move him."

Piper inhaled sharply. "Thank you for the compliment, but all I saw was a man bitterly disappointed because his only son chose to go down another path. I felt desperately sorry for him and thought your parents handled the shock with amazing grace. Everyone did. They couldn't have been kinder."

"He should have kissed you," came the surprisingly wintry comment.

"No, Nic— That would have been asking too much. One day when the killer is caught, you can tell the family everything. By then I'll be long gone and they'll have their son back, free and clear. Now if you don't mind, I'll shower first and get ready for bed."

She undid her suitcase to find her robe and nightgown. On the way to the en suite bathroom she said, "Since you would never fit on the chaise, I'll sleep there tonight."

Nic found extra bedding on the closet shelf and made up the chaise into a bed with a pillow. He put a milk chocolate truffle on top of it, her favorite. Anything to please the bride of his heart.

Tonight she'd passed her first test with better results than he'd dared hope for. He hadn't been kidding her when he'd told her he'd expected his father to walk out of the villa. Explode on the spot and storm out would have been more like it.

But he'd done neither. That was all because he too had been charmed by the last "unexpected" and "astounding" Duchess triplet, as Luc had once called Olivia.

At a distance you didn't realize there was fire hidden beneath their serene blond beauty. But those four days aboard the *Piccione* had proved Piper and her sisters were an amalgam of so many fascinating qualities, neither his life or that of his cousins had been the same since.

Max's phone call last June asking Nic to play captain had resulted in three weddings. But Nic had yet to turn his into a marriage. The time to love his bride into oblivion would come. All he had to do was be patient a little longer.

While he was deep in thought she walked past him in her pink toweling robe, smelling of toothpaste. She picked up the truffle.

"Umm. I love these. Thank you."

"You're welcome."

"I'll save it for tomorrow. I love a piece of chocolate first thing in the morning."

Nic would have to remember that. "Some people would call that decadent."

"I know. Daddy said it was the artiste in me."

He chuckled. "Before we leave for the airport, I'll phone Señor Robles and invite them over for drinks tomorrow evening with the family."

"Good. I have a plan to befriend Camilla and am anxious to try it out."

If a Duchess had a plan, then heaven help the person who got in her way. "I can hardly wait to see my new bride in action."

"I can't wait either. The sooner the monsters who planned that tram accident are behind bars, the sooner I can get back to my life."

Nic felt like someone had just run him through with the sword hanging in the ducal palace war room on the estate.

"That may not happen for a while."

"I know. But I can't rely on Don's good nature to last forever." She lay down on the chaise and pulled the covers over her. "Goodnight, Nic. My sisters tell me I never snore, so you should get a good sleep."

With the mention of Don, plus a comment meant to

be deliberately unromantic, a blackness descended over Nic. If it weren't for the memory of the satisfying way she'd been returning his kisses when he'd forced them on her, he might never sleep again.

The next time his mouth closed over hers, he wouldn't let her go until he sensed in his gut that it wasn't all playacting on her part.

CHAPTER FIVE

MARBELLA, Spain, had the reputation of being the Florida of Europe. According to Nic even in winter it boasted a microclimate of mild winters and more sunny days than anywhere else on the continent.

While Kingston was being hit hard by a new blizzard, Piper had to pinch herself to believe she was really seeing exotic flowers and palm trees beneath a warm sun.

The night of Luc and Olivia's wedding in the estate chapel, she'd asked Max to drive her to the nearest hotel the minute the ceremony concluded. Though Nic's parents had invited everyone to stay over at the ducal palace, a smaller version of the Alhambra she'd visited with Olivia last August, Piper had wanted to get as far away from Nic as possible.

As a result she'd only glimpsed the palace from the limo window. She'd seen nothing of Nic's own villa which Max told her was situated at the foot of the hilly estate on their family's private beach.

It was three in the afternoon by the time the limo bringing them from the Malaga airport wound its way to the water. Through the lush foliage Piper spied her new temporary home, an exquisite, glistening white villa of Spanish and Moorish architecture. The dazzling sight thrilled her to the core of her being.

As Nic helped her from the car, a charming married

couple, Paquita and Jaime, who lived on the estate and were in charge of the staff, came outside to greet them.

When Nic told them Piper was his new bride, they not only hid their shock well, they welcomed her in good English with surprising warmth and acted genuinely happy for him.

While they took care of the bags, Nic could tell how enchanted she was by her surroundings and gave her a quick tour of the villa which was a masterpiece of sculpture itself.

He led her through the clutter-free common rooms, open to the air by means of porticos and breezeways. The sumptuous furnishings and tiled fireplaces created an inviting warmth that made you feel like you were on a permanent vacation.

A secret garden and private terrace off the bedrooms, all alive with flowering plants and trees, added to her entrancement. She gasped in awe when she discovered tiled steps leading down to a rectangular swimming pool. It was lined by rounded arches running the length of the villa. More steps met the sandy beach and the blue Mediterranean beyond.

Southern Spain was an artist's paradise. But few people had entrée to such a spectacular spot on earth as the Pastrana estate, let alone were born to families of royal privilege like the Varano cousins.

While most of the world looked on and marveled, there were those criminals in the world who resented such wealth and killed for it without remorse. Innocent or not, Nina had paid the ultimate price because of her association with Nic. Luc would never ski again because of their unique heritage.

Now that Nic had set the game into motion, Piper was more determined than ever to do her part.

While she stood there mesmerized by a view that masked security guards and lurking danger, Nic emerged from the master bedroom in white swimming trunks. His superb male physique was so physically attractive to her, she had to look away.

"Come and join me in the pool for a swim. Nothing's more relaxing after a plane trip."

With her heart tripping over itself she said, "I think I'll unpack first, then get ready for our guests."

"The Robles family won't be here before seven-thirty this evening. We have plenty of time to lounge."

She sucked in her breath. "In that case I'd like to phone Don and get an update on our latest project."

His eyes grew shuttered. "As you wish. This is your home now. Rearrange my things to accommodate yours, *mi amor*." She wished he would stop calling her "his love." It was as meaningless an endearment as all the others he'd been using. "You must do whatever you like."

Whatever Piper would like?

Run into his arms of course, and never let him go, but he wasn't holding them out to her. No no. She had his cousins to thank for the reason why she'd been chosen for this assignment. Otherwise Consuela Munoz would be here instead and remain his wife for good.

"Thank you."

"I've arranged for you to share office space with me in my library. You'll find a new cell phone on your desk."

"I was planning on buying one. Thank you."

"De nada."

He lifted her suitcase onto the king-size bed for her. Speaking of the bed, that was something else they needed to talk about. Their sleeping arrangements... Whatever they worked out would have to be foolproof so the staff wouldn't gossip.

When she realized Nic was still standing there she muttered, "Enjoy your swim."

"Always. If you change your mind, I'll be waiting."

She didn't respond to his comment, but his words set her body trembling.

By the time she'd made some space for herself in the dresser drawers and closet, Piper heard a splash coming from the pool. She could picture his hard male body doing laps like a torpedo. No telling how long he would stay out there.

Needing to keep her distance from him, she hurried to get everything put away, then wound her way through the villa to his library to phone Don.

Nic's inner sanctum was different from the rest of the house. The large room was lined floor to ceiling with books you reached by a rolling ladder.

She lost track of time studying the hundreds of titles printed in languages in which he excelled. It was the sanctuary of a true scholar. Charts, maps everywhere.

Finally remembering why she'd come in there, she sat down on the adjustable stool of her new drafting table with its own floor lamp. Both pieces of furniture had been placed in front of one of the windows to give her maximum light.

She reached for her new cell phone. There was a

piece of paper underneath with a message written in such beautiful script, she knew it had to be Nic's.

Piper—
This is your new number. I've already programmed your phone with my number first, followed by Greer and Olivia in the number two and three spots.

The owner of the Marbella villa was meticulous and left nothing to chance.

After playing around with her phone for a minute to figure out how it worked, she made her call to New York. For her trouble she got Don's answering machine. She left him her new number and said she would try to contact him again tomorrow.

To her disappointment, her sisters didn't answer their phones either. She gave them her new number before hanging up. On her way out of the library she wandered over to Nic's work area in front of another window.

Alongside the state-of-the-art computer equipment, books and legal pads covered the top of his desk. It was huge and made of fabulous Spanish mahogany. Pulled up to it was an equally impressive deep tufted leather chair inlaid with pounded brass work in the wood reminiscent of the Ottoman empire.

A small framed picture, the only picture on the desk, caught her attention. It was a fascinating photo of Nic and her brothers-in-law on horseback leading a packhorse. They couldn't have been more than twenty years old and had grown beards.

With their overly long hair, the Varano cousins resembled mountain men who'd been away from civilization for a while and were loving it!

She picked it up to examine more closely. Even though they were young and scruffy-looking, they still made a devastating impact. A pain seared her when she thought of all the other women who'd known and loved Nic over those years. Piper would only have been about fourteen at the time this picture was taken.

Had her sisters seen this photograph? Obviously it meant something important to Nic or he wouldn't still keep it on his desk.

"That was taken in Alaska. We went panning for gold."

At the sound of Nic's low voice, she put the picture back down and whirled around, embarrassed to have been caught feasting her eyes on him.

"As if you didn't have enough treasure at home," she teased. "But I guess I have to give you credit for trying to find it by the sweat of your brow. Any success?"

Just then she happened to look up at him dressed in tan trousers and a claret colored Polo shirt. His exciting smile changed the rhythm of her breathing.

"No. The horse carrying our gear got spooked by lightning and took off down the mountain. We spent two days searching before we found him. By then bad weather settled in and we had to stay put. With no food, we must have lost ten pounds a piece."

She laughed. "No wonder you keep the picture for a souvenir. Sometimes when everything goes wrong, those are the best trips in retrospect."

He cocked his head. "Is that your way of telling

me your trip on board the *Piccione* wasn't such a disaster after all?''

Heat suffused her face. ''*What* trip?'' she fired to hide the fact that he'd read her mind with astonishing accuracy.

''You mean that one-way ticket to an Italian prison? Or the time we were kidnapped and held captive in our stateroom? Or could it be the day we escaped on bikes for which we had to pay full price, only to be hauled back to the pier?''

He shrugged his broad shoulders. ''Those were your decisions. We were ready to fulfill your every desire. Why don't you admit you loved being chased as much as we loved chasing you?'' he inserted in a silky voice.

She glared at him. ''Are you crazy? You put the fear in us! We were running for our lives! But you'd have to be a woman to understand, and since you aren't—''

Rich laughter burst out of him. ''No, *mi esposa.* I thank heaven every night that I am not.''

Piper bet he did, especially if he was going to use her for a cover while he started slipping out to be with the woman he loved but supposedly couldn't marry. Since when? So far he'd proved he had a healthy dose of Machiavelli in him too and did exactly what he wanted, when he wanted.

He was just like Luc and Max. The three of them were laws unto themselves!

Unable to tolerate the thought of his being involved with Consuela or anyone else, she started for the door.

''Where are you going?''

''I need to shower and wash my hair.''

''Paquita will serve us a meal on the terrace whenever you're ready.''

"Go ahead and eat without me. I'll probably be a long time blow-drying my hair."

"I'll bring you an adapter for your plug."

He was beginning to remind her of his behavior last June when everywhere she and her sisters turned, he and his cousins showed up without apology.

No sooner had she reached the bathroom than Nic managed to join her. He plugged the device into the socket, then leveled his penetrating brown gaze on her.

They were both dressed, yet she felt ridiculously vulnerable standing so close to him. In a panic, she hurried back in the bedroom where there was more space. Where she could breathe *air*.

"About the sleeping arrangements—" she blurted.

"*Sí?*" came the soft sound directly behind her.

"What are we going to do so the staff doesn't figure out the true situation?"

"We'll go to bed every night in the same bed. We just won't make love."

By now Piper was feeling feverish. Her back was still toward him. "That wasn't part of our arrangement."

"I beg to differ. When you became my legal wife, sleeping with me was implicit in the agreement. Talk spreads, even among my loyal staff. If it will make you feel less pregnable, you're welcome to wear my thermals and ski outfit to bed every night."

On his way out of the room, he paused in the entry. "I have to admit I'm glad to hear you don't snore. To my knowledge, the few women I've had a relationship with haven't complained about me on that score either."

*   *   *

Nic found Paquita sweeping the breezeway. After asking her to make up a tray for his wife, he heard his cell phone ring. He didn't have to look at the ID to know it was his father calling.

Through Luc, Nic had learned that his parents had flown back to Marbella after the party last night. The news didn't come as any surprise. After realizing he had a new daughter-in-law and there wasn't anything he could do about it, Nic's father would have been too restless to stay put.

Nic clicked on. *"Buenas tardes, Papa."*

"I'm on my way to see you. Do me the courtesy of meeting me at my car. Come alone. I'll be in the courtyard within two minutes."

The line went dead.

Nic had known what an enormous shock this had been for his father. If Piper weren't Nic's heart and soul, he would dread this confrontation with him. Not because he feared him, but because it might create an estrangement his stubborn father would let stand.

Over the years Nic had always done everything his parents had wanted him to do, so he felt no guilt over the most important decision of his life. Only an overriding sense of compassion for his father's pain and seeming inability to unbend.

Juan Carlos de Pastrana was a wonderful but rigid man who'd been raised by a father even more rigid. He came by that flaw honestly. In time Nic was counting on Piper's inimitable Duchess spirit to get under his father's skin and win his love.

But it wouldn't happen overnight, and right now Nic's father was feeling anger on behalf of his friend

Benito who'd been counting on an alliance of their two families. Nic was prepared to shoulder all the blame.

However when he walked out of the villa and got in the car with his father who sat at the wheel, he had to admit he wasn't prepared to hear what his parent had to say.

"Either you give up this woman immediately, or I'm renouncing you as my son." *Renouncing?* "You have a half hour to decide. Phone me when you've made your decision."

"You don't mean that, Papa."

Since Nic had always been loyal, his father didn't expect any different behavior from his son now. Unfortunately Nic had no choice but to call his bluff, if it was a bluff...

In case it wasn't, then this meant a true parting of the ways because Piper had become Nic's world. Without her, life made no sense.

"One half hour," his father repeated, his mind inflexible, his lean frame stiff as the body armor worn by his forebearers.

"I don't need time, Papa. I've already made my decision."

"Then I want you off the estate by tomorrow morning and out of my life."

Out of his life?

Nic eyed his father who refused to look at him. "Does Mama know about this?"

"Yes."

Since his father didn't elaborate, Nic knew his mother had to be in despair over the situation. Nic's choice of wife had no doubt brought on the only serious conflict in their marriage.

And conflict it would be because Piper was Nic's wife now, and he had no intention of ever giving her up. He wanted her under all circumstances.

"I'm sorry you feel this way, Papa. I love you very much, but Piper has my heart."

"Get out of the car."

"Before I do that, there's something you should know. In truth I'd hoped never to have to tell you." Nic wouldn't reveal everything. Only enough to open his father's eyes a little wider. "I was never in love with Nina. I had just broken my engagement to her the day she got killed."

The moment the admission was out, his father's head of black hair peppered with gray jerked around in astonishment.

"There's more," Nic asserted. "After our talk, she left the chalet. By chance, Luc saw her rush into the arms of another man before she took the tram ride that ended her life. So it appears that in trying to honor our parents' wishes, neither of us was happy."

His father started to protest, but Nic continued to talk. "You don't have to believe me. Phone your nephew. He was an eye witness and will tell you this man had to be her lover. There could be no other explanation for their passion, or the way they clung to one another."

Silence stretched between them. His father eventually spoke in a gravelly voice. "That doesn't sound like the Nina I knew."

Nic had it in his heart to feel sorry for his parent who'd always thought of Nina as pretty perfect.

"Her liaison with another man came as a surprise to me too. If I hadn't told her my true feelings that day, and there'd been no accident, I have no way of knowing if she would have gone through with our wedding or not.

"Because I knew the news of her relationship with another man would kill Benito and Ynes, I've never said a word to them about it, and I never intend to. But the point I'm making to you is, a union between Nina and me would have ended in disaster, just as a marriage between Camilla and myself would."

His father stirred restlessly in the driver's seat, a sure sign the mention of Camilla had struck a nerve. Obviously this unexpected conversation was causing him great upheaval. That was good. The blinders had needed to come off for years now.

"Though it's never been said out loud, you and I both know Benito and Ynes want Camilla to become a part of our family." His father's head lowered as if in unconscious acknowledgment. "But in the end it will be kinder to her and to them if tonight they find out I already have a new wife."

His father inhaled sharply. "The news could send Benito into cardiac arrest. Are you aware of this?"

"I suppose anything could happen, Papa, but no matter how painful for him, he can't say I didn't honor Nina's memory, can he."

It took a long time before his father finally muttered, "No."

For Juan Carlos de Pastrana to make such an admission was an unprecedented concession.

"Piper is aware they're your best friends. She

knows feelings are going to be fragile for a while, so she's going to do everything in her power to be gracious to them and Camilla.

"If Benito or Ynes dare to express anger over my marriage to her, then they will only be giving themselves away. But you have one consolation. At least if they choose to walk out, it will be from my house, not yours. They will blame me, not you."

Taking a calculated risk Nic added, "Your friendship will remain intact, especially when you tell them you've renounced your only son. That should go a long way to appeasing Benito."

On that salient note, Nic levered himself from the car and shut the door. His father sat there for a few minutes before driving off.

As soon as he did, Nic reached for his cell phone and called Luc. The minute his cousin answered he asked, "Are you alone?"

"Max and I are waiting for the girls. We're about ready to go out to dinner, but we'll be listening for your call no matter how late. We want to hear what happens when your little bomb goes off in front of Señor Robles."

Nic lowered his head. "I'm afraid plans have changed and Father dropped a bomb on me."

"How big?"

"Do you remember last August when you asked me if I would like a permanent neighbor?" That was at a time when Luc believed Olivia was going to marry his brother Cesar, and he didn't think Monaco was big enough to hold the three of them.

"So... Uncle Carlos's performance last night was sheer pretense."

"From start to finish. A few minutes ago he came by the villa with an ultimatum. I just gave him my answer and can still hear the screech of his tires."

"I take it he ordered you to give her up or—"

"Or else he's renouncing me."

"*Renounce?* He went that far?"

"It's the way he's made. I told him I'd chosen my bride, so I have until tomorrow morning to clear out and never come back."

"You're not serious!" Luc let out several colorful French curses.

"Before he drove away, I left him with a lot to think about. Don't be surprised if he calls you for verification."

"About what?"

"Nina's lover."

"You told him everything?"

"No. He's still in the dark about the killer and our suspicions. It's anyone's guess if he'll unbend enough to show up tonight when I face Benito."

"Just a minute, Nic. Max wants to know what's going on." Nic could hear the two of them conversing before his other cousin came on the line.

"I'm sorry Uncle Carlos lost his head, Nic, but these are early days."

"The split with Papa was inevitable, Max. My concern is Piper. The only reason she agreed to marry me was because I told her we needed her to spy on the Robles household for us.

"Depending on how things go tonight, Benito may be too hostile for that plan to work."

"Don't worry. While you get ready for your guests,

Luc and I will come up with another strategy. If the whole thing blows up in your face, then tell Piper you're reverting to Plan B which means that starting tomorrow, you'll be operating from Monaco instead of Marbella.''

"Thanks, Max. As usual, I owe you guys."

"Let's agree we're all permanently indebted to each other. Talk to you later. *Ciao*."

"*Ciao*."

Nic went back inside the villa and found Piper on the terrace finishing the last of the crab salad Paquita had prepared for her. The sight of her freshly washed hair being teased by the breeze stirred his senses as much as the mold of her lovely body in the aqua colored cotton blouse and skirt.

Since last June when he'd first laid eyes on her, he'd longed for the day when she would be ensconced here as his legally wedded wife. What a bitter irony that they might have to leave in the morning.

Her glance lighted on him. "Something's wrong," she spoke without preamble.

"How can you tell?"

"There's a certain set to your jaw. When you're more carefree, your facial muscles are relaxed. The artist in me notices those things."

If he wasn't careful, she was going to notice a lot more.

"Papa dropped by a few minutes ago."

"I figured the events of the coming evening have to be weighing him down."

Nic wrapped his fingers around the back of the chair opposite her. "After considering everything, he's concerned the news of our marriage will come as too great a shock to Señor Robles.''

She pushed herself away from the table and stood up. "He doesn't want us to go ahead with the party this evening, does he."

"No, but we're going to anyway. I'm only telling you this so you won't be surprised if my parents don't make an appearance."

When he could see she was having second thoughts he said, "Shall I get Signore Barzini on the phone to explain why we have to go ahead as planned? This is a case of life and death, and he's leading the investigation. One wrong move could ruin everything."

Piper averted her eyes. "Naturally I wouldn't want to jeopardize the situation, but your father must be sick over what's about to happen."

"Sometimes you have to be cruel to be kind, Piper. Because of Papa's friendship with Benito, for a whole year Camilla has been allowed to believe she'll end up married to me. Do you really think it's fair to her that this be put off a second longer than necessary?"

Her head flew back. "No. Of course not." She shifted her weight. "Do you want me to wear the same suit I had on last night?"

"No. You look perfect the way you are."

"I'm glad you said that. Getting all dressed up would seem like we wanted to flaunt our happiness in their faces."

The innate kindness in Piper bonded her to him in a brand-new way. "My thoughts precisely. As you know from having been introduced to them before, they're very stiff, proper people. Camilla is their offshoot. Seeing us in casual attire will set the tone I wish to convey.''

''You mean that you've married an American beneath your station and are resigned to it.''

''No. That I've married my soul mate and this is the *real* me.''

She smiled her cruel smile. ''You're such a great actor you almost had *me* fooled just now, Captain Pastrana.''

''Am I never to be forgiven for that sin? Your sisters think our undercover personas on the *Piccione* were amusing.''

''My sisters are so much in love with their husbands, they've forgotten there was a time last June when we considered sending for our boyfriends to rescue us from the clutches of three evil Mediterranean playboys.''

Nic grinned. ''You mean Huey, Lewey and Dewey? How were you going to accomplish that miracle?''

''They're in the National Guard and could have caught a military transport to come and get us.''

''I would have liked to see them try,'' he drawled.

''They could have been airdropped in their frogmen suits.''

''Frogmen?'' He laughed.

''Yes. For your information, their specialty is underwater rescue operations. They would have boarded the *Piccione* before Luc could fight them off with his cane.''

More laughter broke from Nic. ''You mean the frogmen versus the dive masters? That's one point for *them*.''

''That wasn't very nice.''

He grinned. "Correct me if I'm wrong, but I seem to recall the Duchess triplets had a one-to-ten scale to measure the men in your lives. The frogmen only came out fours and fives. As I understand it, Max and Luc's ratings ended up scoring way off the chart."

"So did yours," she added unexpectecdly.

A spurt of adrenaline ignited his body. "This is the first I've heard of it."

"Don't get too cocky. It was a chart according to Greer's specifications."

"Meaning yours are different."

"Daddy's *my* chart. So far, no man I've ever known has come close to him."

"You're looking for another father?"

"According to Mother he made a great husband. That's good enough for me."

"Tell me about him."

"How much time have you got?"

"After our party, we've got all night. Were you his favorite?"

"We were all his favorites. That's what made him so wonderful."

"Didn't he ever do anything wrong? Make one mistake?"

"Yes." Nic saw her throat working. "He died."

CHAPTER SIX

PIPER'S emotions were all worked up, threatening to spill over. The dangerous urge to tell Nic she was desperately in love with him was so strong, she needed to do something with her pent-up energy.

"Now that it's getting dark, the temperature has dropped. I'm going inside."

She hurried into the bedroom ahead of him. Before she could reach the hallway, he called to her. "You've forgotten something."

Pausing in the doorway, she turned to him. "What?"

"This."

Nic held up the pearl engagement ring she'd left in the ceramic dish on the dresser. She'd taken it off to wash her hair, and had forgotten to put it back on.

"No bride of mine would be complete without it."

With every step he took toward her, her heart thudded until she could feel its reverberation in her ears. She held out her hand with her palm upward so he could drop it in without touching her.

A small moan escaped when he used both his hands to steady hers and slide it onto her ring finger as he'd done in the limo last evening.

He darted her a searching glance. "You're trembling."

She pulled her hand away, scalded by his touch. "You're not the only person who warned me about

Camilla's volatile disposition. My sisters are afraid she might do me bodily harm when she sees me wearing the ring that used to adorn her sister's finger.''

"You're wrong about the ring, Piper. Nina wore a diamond my father picked out for her from the Pastrana family jewels. I've given you the pearl worn by the Duchess of Parma.''

"Marie-Louise?'' she half gasped the words.

"Who else? This ring was part of the stolen collection that showed up at the auction in London last June. That's where I went after Greer and Max's wedding. I ended up paying a small fortune to recover it.''

Piper shook her head. "I wish you hadn't told me. More than ever I'm afraid of something happening to it. I'm the last person who should be wearing it!'' she cried.

His eyes had a feral gleam. He only looked like that when he was angry. "Who better than the woman who came to Europe the first time wearing the Duchesse pendant? In my opinion, no one has a greater right to it than a blood relative.''

"You said our Duchess family name came from the French spelling, that my family couldn't have descended from the Italian line!''

He pursed his lips. "That was before Signore Rossi discovered there were *two* original Duchesse pendants.

"Napoleon Bonaparte was the Emperor of France. He came by the pearl on his Egyptian campaign. Marie-Louise was his second wife. It's entirely possible the story about one of her female descendents being involved with a monk is true.

"I suspect it was a French monk linked to the Parisian court who spirited the baby and the pendant away to America. One of these years the real truth will come to light.''

''I don't care what the truth is, Nic. This ring belongs back at the ducal palace in Colorno!''

''You mean where another robber won't hesitate to kill in order to steal it again?'' he questioned smoothly, but she heard the undertone of menace. ''I think it's much safer on your hand. Shall we walk through to the other part of the house? Our guests should be arriving soon.''

Piper moved quickly to keep distance between them. To her surprise, Nic's parents were already in the living room enjoying a drink when she entered ahead of him.

Since he'd warned her they might not show up at all, she was doubly relieved to see that Señor de Pastrana had risen to the occasion enough to support his son. As it was, the evening was going to be difficult for Nic to get through.

Though he'd never been in love with Nina, that didn't take away from the fact that he'd been close to the Robles family all his life and didn't relish the thought of hurting them.

After eyeing his father for an overly long moment, she watched Nic hug his mother. They said a few whispered words before she left the warmth of the fire to greet Piper. As they were hugging, she heard voices in the foyer. Soon she saw Nic standing there with the Robles family. The three of them were elegantly dressed and looked the epitome of Spanish aristocratic sophistication.

Camilla had a well proportioned figure and was of medium height like her mother. Her abundance of black hair had been coiled on her head and secured with a mother-of-pearl comb. She wore a stunning burgundy silk dress.

The artist in Piper noticed right away that the color was wrong for her white skin. If she were to wear her hair in short curls around her face, it would soften her features. With the right kind of makeup and younger clothes, she could be very attractive.

While Nic chatted with them in Spanish, Camilla couldn't seem to keep her brown eyes from staring at him. Piper didn't blame her for that. Nic was such a gorgeous male, feminine heads turned in his direction wherever he went. Poor Camilla had been regarding this phenomenon for years.

It must have caused her incredible pain to love him from a distance, knowing all this time he'd been in mourning for her sister.

Nic was right. The sooner Camilla realized he was out of the running, the sooner all that adoration could be showered on another man.

Almost as if he could read her mind, Nic's gaze locked onto Piper's. She heard him say in English, "Camilla? Come in the living room. There's someone important I want to introduce to you. Your parents met her at both of my cousins' weddings."

Nic's mother stayed close to Piper. Señor de Pastrana joined his wife. The scene reminded her of an ancient battlefield with everyone on both sides lined up behind their banners, waiting for the charge to begin.

Piper's breathing turned erratic as Nic moved to her free side. He put a possessive arm around her shoulders.

"This is Piper Duchess, my former cousin-in-law who is now my wife, Señora de Pastrana."

Quiet reigned until Piper wanted to cover her ears.

"You're already married?" Señor Robles whispered in a shaken voice.

"Yes, Benito. It's a long story. After so much unhappiness following Nina's death, I didn't know how I would go on living. For months I grieved. Then I got the phone call from Max that the Duchesse pendants had turned up around the necks of the Duchess triplets from America. He asked for my assistance to carry out an investigation.

"Meeting them was an experience I shall never forget. Their presence was like a ray of sunshine after blinding months of darkness. I watched my cousins fall under their spell. Little did I know during my mourning period that I, too, would be affected by this particular triplet.

"When I was in New York the other day on business, I stopped by to see her at her work. One thing led to another..." Nic's voice faltered.

Piper knew how hard this moment was for him and decided it was time to help him out.

"I—I always prayed Nic would come to see me when his period of mourning was over," she confessed, staring into three pairs of shocked brown eyes. "I couldn't believe it when my assistant told me he was out in the reception area."

Moistening her lips nervously she said, "I fell in love with him on the *Piccione,* but I learned from his cousins he was grieving over Nina. I realized I didn't have the right to expect anything from him, so I went back to New York after Greer's wedding. I only came to Europe one other time, and that was to see Olivia married.''

Her eyes filled with the tears, but she didn't try to hold them back. As long as Nic thought this was a performance, she might just get away with it. If she weren't convincing now, the whole situation would turn into a worse nightmare.

''I had a boyfriend in New York, Tom. He wanted to marry me, and I was on the brink of saying yes when I realized I couldn't go through with it.'' She leveled her gaze on Camilla. ''You can't marry someone you don't love, or who you know doesn't love you.

''Before we broke up, Tom accused me of being in love with Nic. That's when I admitted that I was, but I also told him Nic was in mourning and I would probably never see him again.''

Piper's gaze strayed to Señor Robles whose eyes held a strange glitter. She didn't know how much of it could be attributed to anger or pain. Probably a combination of both now that he realized his hopes of two families uniting had been dashed to pieces.

''When Nic showed up and I knew his period of mourning was over, I'm afraid I was so overjoyed, I left him in little doubt how I felt about him. He transformed my world when he asked me to marry him.

''I was afraid we were in some fantastic dream that was going to disappear. So I called Daddy's best friend and we arranged to be married in his law office. It was the next best thing to having my parents there. They would have loved Nic the way *you* love him.''

She kept dashing the tears from her eyes. ''Nic loves your family so much—'' she blurted. ''He was the one who insisted that we let all of you know the news tonight, before the word spreads.''

Piper took a moment to catch her breath. ''Believe me *Señor* when I tell you that I *know* Nina will always live in Nic's heart. His cousins have indicated she was his great love. But there's room in life for more than one love, don't you think?'' her voice throbbed.

''I love him too,'' she cried softly, ''and I'm going to try to make him as happy as your daughter would have.''

She switched her attention to Señora Robles. ''I hope we can all be friends. I realize I'll never be able to take Nina's place. I've seen pictures of her. She was beautiful, exactly like you and Camilla.''

Some instinct prompted Piper to grasp Ynes's hands. ''Nic tells me his father loves your daughters like his own. Please don't let our marriage change the friendship between your two families.''

Turning to Camilla she said, ''If anything, I want to get to know all of you better. I've been very lost since my parents died and my sisters got married. I'm going to need friends.''

At this point both mothers had started sniffing. Nic's mother handed Piper a handkerchief which she gratefully accepted to wipe the moisture off her face.

The silence coming from the two fathers and Camilla created tension you could cut with a knife, but there was a breakthrough with Ynes. To Piper's joy, the other woman reached out to kiss Piper on both cheeks, then lifted her hands to Nic's face.

''You and your new wife will always be welcome in our home.''

Nic's beautiful dark eyes gleamed with unshed

tears. "Thank you, Ynes. You'll never know what that means to me," he murmured before embracing her.

Benito's movements were stiff, but he finally approached Piper. "Congratulations, Señora de Pastrana." In a gallant gesture, he lifted her left hand that wore the pearl ring, and kissed the top of it.

"Thank you so much, Señor Robles."

At the gesture she saw a relieved expression break out on Nic's father's face. She thanked providence for that much progress.

Nic's hand squeezed her waist hard before he said, "Shall we go into the dining room? I asked Paquita to prepare a light supper for us."

His suggestion brought a grimace to Camilla's features. "I thought we were only coming for drinks. I'm afraid I have other plans for the evening."

When her parents started to protest, Piper smiled at her. "I'm sure you have a special man who's dying to be with you. I can certainly understand why you wouldn't want to hang around here with a bunch of married people. Nic will be thrilled to drive your parents home if you need him to.

"Go on and have a wonderful time. Maybe you'd come over for lunch one day soon? We could swim and talk? I only know about ten Spanish words and need a lot of help."

"Of course she will," Ynes spoke up when her daughter didn't say anything.

"I'll see you out to the car, Camilla," Nic offered. He knew Nina's sister was in shock. If Piper had been in her shoes, she would have wanted to bolt too. Who could blame her?

Camilla said her goodnights to everyone, then disappeared into the foyer with Nic.

Piper turned to the others. "They'll probably want to talk for a few minutes. Why don't we go in the dining room and get started? Nic will join us when he's ready."

She thought he would be a long time, but he returned before the fish soup had been served to everyone. He took his place next to Piper. The next thing she knew, he'd reached underneath the table to squeeze her thigh. She presumed it was his way of thanking her, but she wished he'd chosen another method and would remove his hand.

The heat sent tendrils of delight unfurling through her body. Sensitive to the Robles's feelings, Nic hadn't been demonstrative to Piper in front of them. But this was almost worse because she couldn't run away or tell him to stop what he was doing.

Conversation got around to the paintings Piper had brought to Europe with her. Nic's mother made a lot of flattering remarks about them.

Nic drained his wineglass. "Piper's a brilliant artist. When I first became familiar with her work, I had no idea she did portraits. Not until I entered her apartment in New York and saw one of her parents hanging on the wall. It was a masterpiece."

Piper blinked. She had no clue he'd paid that much attention.

Señor de Pastrana spoke up for the first time. He was looking at Benito. "Your birthday is next month. The first thing I'd like to ask of my new daughter-in-law is to paint you and Ynes as one of our gifts to you."

"I'd be honored," Piper cried softly. "Nic says you have the most exquisite villa in Andalusia, Señor Robles. Maybe you could pose in one of your favorite rooms or on the grounds while I work up a few drawings. Someplace where there's enough light to bring out the gloss in your hair."

"My hair?" he questioned in surprise.

"Yes. It's been said a woman's hair is her crowning glory, but the Spanish men can claim the same thing. With your dark eyes and marvelous bone structure, the Andalusian people have the most wonderful coloring and faces I've ever seen."

By now Nic's handprint had to be emblazoned on her leg before he eventually let her go.

"Perhaps your daughter-in-law would like to paint you and Maria first," Benito murmured to his old friend, but Piper could tell he'd been pleased by the whole idea.

"Piper will get around to painting my parents one day." Nic got to his feet and walked over to the sideboard. "We have the rest of our lives, so there's no doubt of it. Cognacs everyone?"

Nic did the honors.

"None for me," Piper whispered when he would have poured one for her.

The drinks signaled the end of the meal. Nic's parents offered to drive their friends home. Nic walked them out to the courtyard. No sooner did he come back inside the foyer and shut the door than he grabbed Piper.

"Nic—put me down. What are you doing?"

He swung her around and around like they were on a dance floor. Finally he lifted her above him. His eyes were alive with excitement. She'd never seen him this animated before.

"You did it!

"My father and Benito are still speaking to each other. In fact I have a feeling they're going to be closer than ever. Only a Duchess could have pulled off such a fantastic coup. Come on, *mi corazón*."

Handling her as if she were light as air, he lowered her to his shoulder in a fireman's lift.

"Where are we going?" she demanded. He'd started for the other part of the villa.

"For a conference to plot out our next strategy."

"Where?"

"In the pool."

"It's too cool out."

"Not for the woman who's half fish. I won't take no for an answer. There'll be a treat for you if you beat me into the water."

"And a trick if I don't?"

He only laughed that deep male laughter. It seeped into every atom of her body, driving her to change into her swimsuit in record time. Still, he was the one treading the shimmery water in the center of the heated pool when she surfaced from her dive.

The soft lights from the arcaded columns threw his distinctive masculine features into striking relief. With his powerful arms spread wide, and his white smile so captivating it was sinful, Piper didn't know how to shield herself against her intense attraction to him.

"If it weren't for your confession of love in front of both families, the news of our marriage would have started the 100 Years War, Spanish style."

"I'm so glad everything worked out, that your par-

ents didn't stay away after all. Your father's suggestion that I paint Nina's parents was inspirational.''

"Your remarks were so flattering, Benito didn't
want to throw down the gauntlet. That's because my
disarming wife made everything sound like it came
straight from your heart. Even *I* believed you," his
voice rasped.

"That's good," she said in her steadiest tone. "I
intend to do whatever it takes to prevent another murder that could devastate our families forever."

His smile began to fade. "Nothing's going to happen to any of us."

Piper did a somersault to get hold of her emotions.
When she came up for air, Nic was right beside her.

"What's wrong?" he whispered.

"Camilla. She's the wild card. I saw the way she
was looking at you tonight."

Water dripped off his firm, square chin. "It was
difficult to read her thoughts, yet you handled her like
a pro. No one could think you knew anything about
her father's plans for her."

While Nic was speaking, his veiled gaze roved over
her features and curves before traveling the length of
her limbs. Talk about reducing her to a liquid state!
Somehow she had to pretend she didn't notice the way
he was looking at her.

He was a man after all. In fact he was a married
man who'd told her he'd be willing to make their marriage real if it was what she wanted. Right now her
body was so feverish for wanting him, she was in danger of forgetting her pride and giving in to her needs.

But in the morning she would wake up to the reality
that he was in love with someone else. No amount of

lovemaking in the night would make up for that stark fact.

No Duchess worth her salt would sell her soul in that way, not even if she had a piece of paper to prove she was married.

Piper flipped onto her back and propelled herself around with a few strong kicks. Nic stayed with her.

"Piper?"

At the sound of her name she stopped swimming and treaded water. "What is it?" Her pulse raced. "Do I feel a trick coming on?"

He smiled. "Not a trick. When I walked both families to the car, I invited them to witness our wedding ceremony in the estate chapel tomorrow at sunset."

She started to panic. "Surely that's not necessary—" In her hearing Nic had told Mr. Carlson it would happen, but she'd been positive it would never come to this!

She swam to the edge of the pool where she heaved herself up on the tile. He followed with lightning speed and grasped her feet. She thought at first he was going to pull her in. But instead he made soft little circles with his thumbs on her insteps. His sensual touch threatened to put her in an erotic trance.

"It's part of the plan outlined by Signore Barzini. Our marriage must be solemnized by the church. It will convince both families that ours is a love match.

"The blessing of the priest will set the seal on our life together, and bring about a new peace between my father and Benito. All of that has to take place for you to eventually gain Camilla's confidence. As for your sisters, they would expect nothing less."

Nic always made sense, but every minute spent with

him seemed to weave her more inextricably into his life. When it came time for parting, how was she going to bear it?

"Do you want to phone them now and invite them to witness the ceremony, or shall *I* get my cousins on the line?"

She inched back from the edge, forcing him to relinquish her feet. "I'll call them."

He levered himself onto the tile and rose to his full, intimidating height. "While you contact them, I'll use my cell phone in the library to talk to the priest and make the necessary arrangements. Go ahead and use the shower first."

Piper hurried inside to do his bidding. Her body trembled while she stood beneath the spray, but it was out of fear, not cold. Tomorrow night at this time she would be married to Nic in the eyes of God and the church. This role she'd agreed to play had gotten way out of hand.

After drying herself off, she slipped on a nightgown and her terry-cloth robe. It might not be a ski outfit, but the thick material covered her from neck to ankle. With her damp hair, she wasn't the most enticing figure in the world, and that was the way she wanted to keep it.

She took her cell phone from the dresser and phoned Greer first. It was crazy, but she did it by instinct. You'd think after all this time she would have broken the habit of the middle sister deferring to the older sister syndrome...

"Hello?"

"Hi Greer. It's *moi*."

"Thank heaven. Since we got back from dinner,

we've been sitting out on Luc's terrace waiting for you or Nic to call and tell us what happened tonight. The guys have worn a hole in the tiles and Olivia thinks another bout of morning sickness is coming on.''

''Tell her everything went amazingly well considering the circumstances. Camilla left early on her own, but Nic's father and Señor Robles went home friends. As Nic said, major war has been averted.''

''That's the best news we could have.''

No. There could be better news. Like the fact that the killer was caught, and Nic was madly in love with Piper instead of someone else.

''I agree.''

''Just a minute while I give everyone an update. They're all dying to hear details.''

Before Greer came back on the line, Piper shuddered in reaction to think how ghastly it would have been if things had gone the other way.

''Hi. I'm back. Luc was just saying that anyone can see how in love you two are. Uncle Carlos's heart would have to be made out of stone not to be accepting.''

Nic was the best con artist around if he could fool Greer. ''It was Señora Robles who broke the ice and kissed me first.''

''You're the peacemaker, Piper. I knew you'd be able to pull it off and win those difficult men around. I'm so happy for you and Nic. Already Olivia's feeling better.''

''I hope that's true because I'm calling for a specific reason. Nic and I are going to be married in the chapel tomorrow evening.''

''That's even better news. We'll fly to Marbella in

the morning and help you get ready. Do you have a wedding dress?''

Her fingers tightened on the receiver. ''I thought I'd wear the white chiffon I was married in.''

''No, Piper. That's not good enough for your husband,'' she said in a hushed tone. ''Tomorrow we'll go shopping and find you the most gorgeous dress on earth. Something to give Nic a heart attack when he sees you walking to the altar.''

She struggled for breath. In order to give your husband a heart attack, he had to be in love with you, but she couldn't say anything like that to Greer. Not now.

''I'd love some help.'' Tears caused her throat to close up. In truth she'd missed her sisters horribly since last August. Though Dr. Arnavitz had given her wonderful advice, work wasn't everything. ''I can't wait to spend some more time with you and Olivia.''

''We feel the same way. Nothing's been right with you living in New York. It's all for one, and one for all, remember.''

''How could I ever forget?'' she laughed through the tears.

''Once we're together, we can really talk and you can tell us everything that happened,'' she continued to whisper. ''We want to know all about Camilla's reaction.''

''Yeah, well, there's quite a bit to report in that department.''

''I'll just bet. So—'' She resumed her normal speaking voice. ''Now that the gorgeous, three tongued Don Juan de Pastrana is off the market for good, how does it feel to be the one responsible for such a catch?''

I wish I knew...

"I'm still kind of in shock."

"I know what you mean. Sometimes when I look at Max and realize he's my husband, I can't believe it either. Did I tell you I'm more in love with him than ever?"

"I kind of figured that. Max must be standing right next to you."

"He is. Mom and Dad would be crazy about our husbands. You should see how sweet Luc is to Olivia, especially now that she's pregnant. When we first met him on the *Piccione,* could you have imagined the day dawning that we would ever call him sweet?"

Don't get me started, Greer.

Luc was besotted. So was Max. Nic was a different story.

She cleared her throat. "Not any more than I can imagine that you used to call Max the great black."

"Hmm...sometimes he still deserves the title."

"Did I tell you I've started another calendar entitled Unpolitically Correct Animals Of The Mediterranean? There's a great black Italian shark I've named Maximilliano featured for June. All the female sharks are in love with him, but he keeps swimming around after the elusive, sleek blond dolphin called Pansy Eyes who refuses to give him the time of day."

Greer chuckled before Piper heard her tell the others. There was a burst of laughter.

"Luc feels left out," she said when she came back on the line.

"Tell him not to worry. August's selection is Lucien the Monagasque octopus with the injured tentacle. All the female octopi fight over who gets to care for him, but he's only interested in the svelte blond dolphin with the sapphire eyes who moves too fast for him.''

''I can't wait to see your drawings. Just a minute,'' she said in order to relate the last to the others. More laughter ensued.

''Am I in your book too?'' came a husky voice.

CHAPTER SEVEN

NIC—

How long had he been standing there? Piper's head swerved in his direction.

"Of course. You and the cast of thousands from that good-old-boy network who prevented us from enjoying our Riviera trip."

Nic's eyes gleamed with amusement. "You mean Signore Galli, the head of security at Genoa airport, is in there?"

"Of course. He's January's selection. The pompous barracuda guarding the entry to Genoa harbor is holding three unsuspecting blond dolphins captive.

"And of course there's the police shore patrol who plucked us out of the water at Lerici, the prison warden in Colorno who refused to hear our case, the jailer who laughed at me, Mr. Carlson who helped Max close ranks on us. Need I go on?"

He folded his arms. "What kind of a fish did you make me out to be?"

"Nicolas the Andalusian sting ray whose whiplike tail can spurt venom in six different languages. You were the perfect choice for February, the month of romance. Though the female sting rays follow you around, they know to keep their distance after you frightened off a defenseless blond dolph—"

"Piper? Oh Piper— I'm still here—"

Uh-oh.

Embarrassed, she spoke into the phone once more. "Sorry, Greer. Nic just walked in and naturally he wanted to hear all about himself. Go figure." She chuckled as she said it, but for some reason, Nic wasn't smiling anymore.

"It's getting late," Greer said. "I'm sure my new brother-in-law wants you all to himself so I'll say goodnight."

"I don't need to hang up yet."

"Yes you do."

Greer was right. Nic's whole mood had changed to something forbidding. "Tell Olivia goodnight for me. See you guys tomorrow."

"We'll be there in the morning. Ten-thirty at the latest."

"I'll be ready. Goodnight."

"Ready for what?" Nic demanded when she hung up.

"The girls and I are going shopping for my wedding dress."

For a moment she thought her comment had appeased him until he asked, "Whose idea was that?"

She got up from the side of the bed. "Greer's," Piper said with the greatest of pleasure. "She's trying to be my mother right now. So far this charade is working. My sisters believe we're really in love. I thought that was what you wanted, but evidently something's wrong."

"Nothing could be more right," he clipped out. "I've just spoken with the priest. Our wedding will go ahead as scheduled. My aunts and uncles will be here to celebrate with us."

"But you're still upset about something." She

frowned. "Has there been a new development in the case?"

"Not to my knowledge."

"Then what's bothering you?"

"I don't know that I like being compared to a sting ray."

"Why not?" she fired, pretending to take him at face value. But she'd lived around him for the better part of a week and was getting to know his various moods. Something significant was going on inside him he had no intention of sharing with her. At least not yet. "They're one of the ocean's most awesome creatures."

"Awesome could be translated...unapproachable," he theorized.

So her comment rankled him. That made her happy.

"When God created the fish, he gave them their own defense mechanisms. The ability to repel was the whole idea with the sting ray."

"Piper," his voice grated. "The afternoon following Max's wedding, I didn't reject you because I wanted to."

Her body froze. "I know exactly why you did what you did. The chivalrous son of the Duc de Pastrana was honoring his courtly commitment."

His lips thinned, but she kept on talking. "It sent up an impenetrable shield to camouflage the fact that you've been in love with someone else all this time."

After a slight pause he said, "That's true, but you're the last person I would ever want to hurt."

His brutal honesty cut her like a glass shard.

"I'll admit it stung my pride. Pardon the pun. But as you can see, there was no permanent damage done.'' She bestowed a fulsome smile on him. ''Living with you, I've found out you're going to make the most terrific cousin-in-law in the world...once our marriage is annulled of course.''

His mouth twisted unpleasantly. ''Aren't you getting ahead of yourself?''

''I hope not. I've got a business to run back in New York. Why don't you hurry and get ready for bed so we can talk about what would be the best way for me to approach Camilla.''

''I'm not sure what that is. She threw me a curve tonight.''

Piper's heart skipped a beat. ''What kind?''

''I'll join you in a minute and tell you.''

That sounded ominous.

Feeling off balance, Piper climbed under the covers. By the time he turned out the lights and got in on the other side, she'd made certain her back was toward him.

When he didn't immediately speak, she found herself prodding him for an explanation.

''If you want to know the truth, Camilla said the last thing I expected to hear.''

Forgetting their proximity, she turned on her other side so she could see his face. The momentum practically had her rolling into him. On a soft moan she squiggled away and sat up.

''W-what did she tell you?''

Nic lay on his back in a T-shirt and sweats, his hands behind his head. But he was still too close for her equilibrium to handle. ''After I invited her to attend our wedding ceremony tomorrow evening with her parents, she said she would love to come. Then she kissed my cheek and thanked me for getting her off the hook with her parents.''

Piper pursed her lips. ''That *was* unexpected. I'm not sure I believe her though. With her kind of pride, it may have been the only thing she could think of to save face with you.''

''Maybe. Maybe not.''

''Are you saying Camilla has been playacting in front of both families for the last year?''

''I don't honestly know.''

Piper's thoughts were reeling. ''Is she the type who would pretend to be amenable to her parents' expectations? Does that streak of honor run as deeply in her as it does in you?''

''I wasn't honorable,'' his voice grated. ''My engagement to Nina was a lie from start to finish.''

''An honorable lie then. If the same is true of Camilla, then the news of our marriage has freed her to be herself. It would be bad enough for her to be in love with you knowing you didn't love her. But to have to marry you when she believed you'd been madly in love with her sister— I can't even imagine it.''

He made a noise in his throat. ''It would never have happened.''

''If she really meant what she said tonight, do you think the situation will make her more or less friendly toward me?''

''We'll find out when you start the portrait my father has asked you to do. Next week I'll give Benito a call to set things up.''

''Next week— Why not sooner?''

''Because both families will assume we want as

much private time as possible together. They would be shocked if we allowed the world to intrude before this week was even out.''

Nic's logic couldn't be refuted. She had no choice but to go along with it.

He moved onto his side toward her, almost overpowering her with his potent male aura. ''That was very clever of you to suggest using their villa for a backdrop.''

His proximity made her heart jump around. She resumed her former position away from him.

''Most people are more comfortable being painted in their own homes. Maybe I can suggest that Camilla be in the painting with them.''

''Excellent idea, *mi esposa.*''

His wife. What a joke.

''We'll see. Even if she refuses to be a part of it, she might hang around to watch. However I'm not holding out any hope that she'll warm up to me.''

''Perhaps that is asking too much, but I'm counting on her curiosity about you to get the best of her.''

''I'm a curiosity all right. The antithesis of Nina. No doubt she and Camilla were confidantes. Nina wouldn't have been able to keep her affair with Lars a complete secret. Women have to talk, especially sisters if they're close in age.''

''So I've discovered since I met the irrepressible Duchess triplets,'' Nic drawled. ''Now that you've returned to the European continent, my cousins are going to have to put up with sharing their wives again.''

Nic's truculent mood seemed to have dissipated for the moment.

''That's right. Women chat. Men react.''

He chuckled. "I don't think that slogan was on any of your calendars I've seen."

"It's not."

"How come?"

"Because I just made that one up. Now you understand why the slogans were Greer's department."

"Why do you always let her be in charge?"

"Because long ago Olivia and I learned Greer's always right."

His chuckling grew louder.

"Laugh all you want. You're an only child so you've never had to figure out your place in the family constellation. Being a triplet complicates it even more."

"Being the only child has its own complications. Trying to fulfill your father's every wish for you comes at a price."

Her eyes smarted when she thought of his burden.

"Touché. I've decided to do you a favor and stop talking. Even the restless sting ray needs some quiet time. Goodnight, Nic."

"That's the one!"

Both Piper's sisters sounded so decided, she knew she'd come to the end of her search.

Surrounded by floor-length mirrors, she looked at herself again. The heavy peau-de-soie wedding dress flared from the waist with a medium-size train embroidered in lace and pearls. It had cap sleeves and a rounded neck. She looked like a princess, but she'd never felt less like one.

"It's the exact color of your pearl."

"What am I going to do for a veil?"

"Your gown's Italian, so you need something Spanish. I know—" Olivia made excited sounds. "I'll be right back."

"How come you're so nervous," Greer demanded once they were alone.

"I'm not."

"Yes you are. You're all flushed and uptight. Are you sure you got married in New York?"

"Greer—"

"I was only teasing. But you have to admit you're acting like this is your wedding day. You know what I mean."

"That's ridiculous. I've been an old married lady for three days now."

"Then how come you guys aren't off on your honeymoon? You could have had one before coming back to face everyone."

Piper turned away from her sister. "You know how proper Nic is."

"Not when it comes to getting what he really wants. He wanted you and ended his formal mourning period a week early to go after you. So what happened?"

"Nothing happened!"

"You're forgetting I can see your face in the mirror. You're lying through your teeth. We're your sisters. You can tell us anything."

"Please tell us what's wrong," Olivia implored. She'd come back in the dressing room carrying a floor-length lace mantilla in her arms. "You've been snapping all morning. It isn't like you."

"I'm sorry."

Olivia motioned to Greer. Together they placed the

mantilla over her head, making sure it fell evenly to the floor on all sides.

"Nic's going to have a heart attack when he sees you."

A church wedding.

She couldn't go through with it.

"What's the matter, Piper?" Both of them caught hold of her.

"You went white just like I do when I feel morning sickness coming on," Olivia murmured compassionately.

"I—I forgot to eat breakfast."

Greer shook her head. "That's not why you're sick. Come on. Tell us the truth. We know you're not pregnant. We also know you and Nic are crazy about each other. So why aren't you deliriously happy?"

She swallowed hard, avoiding their inquisitive eyes. "I just don't see the necessity of getting married again."

"But we want to see you say your vows," Olivia reasoned.

"We've said them already!"

"Not in church." Trust Greer to zero in on the enflamed spot. Her delicate brows formed a frown. "Why does the thought of a church wedding frighten you?"

"Did I say that?" Piper lashed out.

"Is it true?" Olivia questioned. "Are you worried your marriage isn't going to last?"

"That's it!" Greer nodded. "What makes you think you won't be with Nic forever? Does Camilla have something to do with this?"

"No!"

"That was too emphatic. Has she threatened you in some way?"

"No— I— It's not what you think."

"Then tell us, because we're not leaving this fitting room until we've heard the whole truth."

Piper lifted her head. She couldn't keep her secrets any longer. With tears streaming down her cheeks she said, "It's h-horrible you guys. I mean more horrible than you can imagine."

Her sisters must have believed her. "We can't talk here. You'll stain your dress. Come on. We'll ask the saleswoman to get everything ready and we'll come back later."

While Greer removed the mantilla, Olivia started the unbuttoning process down her back. Piper put on her cream suit with the aqua piping, then hurried out to Nic's black sedan ahead of them.

By the time her sisters joined her, she'd pulled herself together enough to tell them everything.

With each shocking revelation, their expressions darkened until she hardly recognized them.

"They could have all been murdered in that tram accident," Olivia's voice shook, "and now *you're* in danger."

"Don't worry. Nic has hired security to protect all of us on a twenty-four hour basis."

"What do you mean 'all'? We're being watched too?" Greer questioned.

"Yes."

"Right now?"

"Yes."

She shook her head. "Nic had no right to ask this of you, not when the police have proof this Lars killed

Nina. Now that you're his wife, this monster could come after you!''

"Nic didn't put a gun to my head.''

"In a way he did," Greer muttered coldly. "He knew you would fly to our rescue. I can't believe our husbands have kept this from us.''

"That's because they love you so much and don't want you worried about anything. Think about this for a minute. Would either of you have done any less if you'd been in my shoes?''

The three of them stared at each other for a long time without saying anything because they all knew the answer to that question.

"Don't be angry at them or Nic. He can't help it that he's in love with someone else. At first I didn't believe him, but looking back now, if he'd really loved me, he would have done something about it on the day you got married, Greer. Certainly on our first wedding night.

"That's why I dread this fake ceremony in the chapel. Signore Barzini who's the head of the investigation insists it's necessary. But when we say our vows in front of the priest, I'll know Nic's will be lies. As soon as this Lars and any accomplices are arrested, we'll be getting an annulment.''

"He really hasn't tried to make love to you? Not even last night?'' Greer's eyes looked pained.

"No, and I gave him every chance. All he had to do was reach out a few inchcs in the night and I would have gone up in flames. I guess the question is, will I be forgiven for taking vows in the church when I know they're meaningless to him?''

"Of course you'll be forgiven you silly goose," Olivia assured her.

"That's not the point," Greer declared. "Nic used you to wiggle out of the hold his father has always had on him. Now he expects you to spy for him."

"Greer— I agreed to everything because I love him, so let's not go there. Now that I've unburdened myself, I feel much better. When we get back to the villa, you guys have to put on the performance of your lives by pretending you know nothing about this. Do you swear to keep silent?"

"We swear," they said in unison.

"That's good because Nic loves you two. He's promised me nothing's going to happen to any of you and I believe him. In his own way, he's a very noble man, like a chivalrous knight of old.

"Another man might have taken advantage of the situation. Nic is true blue to his own code of honor. The woman he's crazy about is the luckiest person on earth."

"Do you have any idea who it is?"

"It's either some married woman, or his editor Consuela Munoz."

For the first time in their lives, Greer broke down and cried in front of her and Olivia. "How could Nic not love you? I can forgive him anything but that. You're the most wonderful, selfless, kind, loyal person."

Piper couldn't believe it. Her older sister was actually crying over her. It warmed her heart.

"Don't be upset for me. One day I'll meet the right man who'll love me the way Max and Luc love you guys. It'll happen. You didn't really expect the Husband Fund to work three miracles did you?"

By now Olivia was in tears. They both tried to laugh, but couldn't. Oddly enough Piper felt much better since she'd been able to unload. She was the only dry-eyed triplet left.

"I'll run in and get my wedding dress. Be right back."

"You're going to need help." After wiping their eyes, her sisters got out to join her inside the bridal shop. Once they'd packed everything in the car, Greer turned to Piper.

"Do you have a ring for Nic?"

"No. That would have made everything seem too real."

"Considering this is a matter of life and death, you *have* to make this ceremony look as real as possible. I saw a jewelry store about a mile back on the same street."

"I remember it." Olivia started the car. She'd always been their designated driver because she had the best sense of direction. Piper got in front with her, Greer in the back. They pulled away from the curb and joined the mainstream of traffic.

Parking was impossible in the heart of Marbella. Olivia said she would drive around the block while Piper got out and hurried inside the jewelry store.

When she told the jeweler she wanted a man's wedding band that matched the gold filigree of her own ring, he started to act very strange. "Where did you come by this pearl ring?"

Uh-oh. Piper had no choice but to tell him she was Señora de Pastrana, the new bride of Nicolas de

Pastrana. "He recovered the stolen ring from the Marie-Louise collection. Now I want to purchase a matching band for my husband to surprise him."

At that point the jeweler couldn't have been more overjoyed. She was given the royal red carpet treatment and walked out of the store with a band that could have been a match for the other.

When she got back in the car, Olivia flashed her a glance. "Greer and I want to treat you to a pre-wedding brunch at Puerto Banus. Last month Nic took us to a restaurant called Pedro's Beach. The best seafood I ever tasted. What do you say?"

Piper was so glad her sisters knew the truth of everything, she'd regained her appetite. "I'd love it."

Nic wouldn't even notice how long she was gone. She imagined he and his cousins were on the phone with Signore Barzini, telling him about last night's developments. Plotting.

They reached the harbor with its gleaming white oceangoing yachts set against a backdrop of mountains. Olivia pointed to one in the distance called the *Juan-Carlos*. "That's the Pastrana yacht. It's fabulous."

Of course. Anything to do with Nic or his cousins approached the surreal.

Olivia seemed to have magic radar to know where to find parking in the crowded areas hugging the beach.

She finally snatched a spot and turned off the motor. As Piper reached for the door handle she saw something that shocked her so much she cried, "Guys—don't get out of the car yet!"

They stared at her in surprise.

"Look at that couple on the pier next to the yacht called the *Britannia*. Their arms are draped around each other. It's Camilla and Lars! Nic showed me pictures of him. With that build and hair color, the two men have to be the same person."

Olivia gasped. "Oh my gosh…"

"What?" Piper and Greer said at the same time.

"It's the same guy who tried to get me to go to a discotheque with him in Monterosso last August! I remember now. His name was Lars!"

"Are you sure?" Piper cried.

"Positive! He was with a group of German and Croatian guys." Her face paled. "They got me involved in a game of Frisbee. I did it to make Luc jealous, but I could tell Lars was on the make so I swam back to the *Gabbiano*. He came after me and grabbed my leg while I was climbing the ladder, but Luc frightened him off."

Greer's brows knit together in a fierce frown. "Do you think he'd been following you and Luc?"

"No. He was on the beach and couldn't have known I would ask Nic to sail the boat in there at the last second."

"I bet Monterosso is the hangout for that gang of killers," Piper speculated. "It isn't far from Colorno where the collection was stolen."

"Guys— Lars is going aboard the *Britannia*. Camilla's starting to walk toward the parking lot. Put your heads down," Greer cautioned.

Every few seconds Piper lifted her head just enough to track the other woman's progress. After a few minutes she saw Camilla drive away in a dark blue car.

"Okay. She's gone." Her sisters sat up.

Piper looked at both of them. "I have to phone Nic and tell him what I saw, but I don't want him to know that *you* know anything. He swore me to secrecy."

"No problem," Olivia exclaimed. "We've got body-guards protecting us as we speak, right?"

"Yes. Let me talk to him before we start driving so he'll think I'm alone."

They nodded.

Piper pulled out her new cell phone and pushed the first digit.

"We put candles in the niches. Everything is ready for the ceremony, Señor de Pastrana."

Nic shook the florist's hand. "I appreciate your help. My bride loves roses and begonias. She'll be especially pleased with the way you've arranged the flowers."

"*Gracias.*"

The men got in their van and drove away. He locked the chapel doors. After climbing in his sports car, he discovered that the cell phone he'd left on the seat was ringing. He checked the Caller ID. It was his wife.

"Piper? Are you and the girls bac—"

"Nic— Listen to me—" she whispered. He had a hard time hearing her.

"The girls think I'm having a private chat with my new husband because I can't stand to be apart from you."

While Nic reacted to the pain inflicted by another debilitating salvo, he heard, "I'm calling from the parking lot of Pedro's Beach restaurant where we were going to eat lunch, but it's too crowded so we changed our minds.

"Nic? Lars is in Puerto Banus."

Her news almost caused him to drop the phone.

"Camilla's with him. They were standing next to a medium-size yacht called the *Britannia,* and acting very much like lovers. Now he's gone aboard and she has driven off."

At those words Nic felt an adrenaline rush. "Do you think you were spotted?"

"No. There are too many people around."

"Thank God for that. Get out of there and drive straight to the villa. I'll see you at home in a few minutes."

Once he'd phoned Signore Barzini with the latest news, he took off for the villa where Max and Luc were doing laps in the pool.

The second they heard about Lars and Camilla, they climbed out of the water for a conference.

"The girls will be here any minute. We don't have much time," Nic explained. "It's my opinion Lars used Nina in order to steal the Marie-Louise collection. I think she was an innocent pawn. When he couldn't learn any more information from her about the Pastrana diamonds, he got her out of the way and went to work on Camilla."

Lines furrowed Max's forehead. "When he's through using her, she'll be expendable too."

Luc tossed the towel he'd been using on a chair. "If Camilla believes Lars is in love with her, then she probably rushed to tell him she's free to marry him."

"Her visit means he knows Piper and I are being married in a private ceremony this evening."

Max nodded. "If he's been lying in wait on the *Britannia* for the right time to steal the jewels, tonight would be the perfect opportunity. We'll all be assembled in the chapel."

"Yes," Nic said with a diabolical smile. "While the wedding goes ahead as scheduled, there'll be a welcoming committee ready to greet Lars at the palace. If he doesn't come, the police are tracking him on the yacht.

"Before the girls get here, let's go in the library and make the necessary calls to set plans in motion."

Among other things, Nic needed to check with Luc on the final details for his honeymoon. *There wasn't going to be an annulment.*

A few minutes later he heard voices in the foyer alerting him the girls were back. Nic walked out to help Piper by carrying the garment bag to their bedroom.

Once the door was closed, she took it from him and hung it in the closet. When she emerged, she said, "Do you think the police have already taken Lars into custody? If so, we can call off the wedding."

He sucked in his breath. "That's the one thing we can't do. Because of you, *mi amor,* the police have been given their first real break in this case, and are setting up a sting operation for tonight."

"You're kidding!"

"No. While our ceremony goes off as planned with everyone we love safely assembled in the chapel, Signore Barzini is hoping to catch Lars and his band of thugs in the act of stealing the Pastrana diamonds from Papa's secret hiding place in the palace."

"What if he doesn't come?"

"The yacht has been put under surveillance. One way or another, they're going to catch him now. You'll be hailed as a heroine, not only by the family, but by international law enforcement."

"I'm no heroine. I just want to go back to New York."

"Well it won't be happening tonight."

She studiously avoided his eyes. "Obviously not."

He watched her fumble for something in her purse.

"Here— As long as there's going to be a ceremony, you need to find out if it fits so I won't make a fool of myself trying to shove it on your finger."

He took the tiny box from her and opened it to find a man's wedding band inside, but it was different from anything he'd ever seen. She'd picked out a ring of gold filigree similar to the filigree of her ring.

"Of course if ours were a true marriage, I would have paid for it with my own money," came the first of more slings and arrows meant to vivisect him. She was succeeding...

"Since this is all part of a con, you're going to be getting the bill. A big one I'm afraid because the jeweler recognized the Parma pearl. I knew he was about ready to call the police, so I had to tell him I'm your wife, and that you'd recovered part of the stolen Marie-Louise collection from a London auction.

"The dollar signs in his eyes almost blinded me. Sorry to do that to you, but Greer insisted I buy a ring for you. Like I said, she's trying to take Mother's place.

"Luckily there was so much traffic, I told the girls to drive around the block while I went inside the shop, so they don't know I didn't pay for it. But there's one good thing.

"They insisted that my wedding dress was their gift to me since my mom couldn't be here to do the honors. You won't be getting a bill for that, thank goodness."

While she chattered on and on, Nic slid the ring on his finger. She might still be fighting him, but the fact that she'd picked out something singularly unique to match her own ring made his heart leap.

"It's a perfect fit. I will always cherish it."

"You'd better give it back to me before we both forget and you show up wearing it ahead of time."

He removed it. "Do you want to practice putting it on me right now?"

"Don't be absurd." Color filled her cheeks as she snatched it from his palm and put it back in the box. Her reactions were growing more and more interesting. "As long as you didn't have any trouble getting it on, I'm not worried. How soon do we have to leave for the chapel?"

"By five. The ceremony's set for five-thirty."

"That's two hours away. I think I'll join my sisters in the pool before they help me get ready."

"Excellent idea. It will give me time to shower and dress first. Since you missed breakfast and lunch, I'll ask Paquita to bring you a meal on the terrace."

"Thank you."

She wheeled around and rushed to the bathroom. While he was speaking to his housekeeper, Piper reappeared wearing her swimsuit and a towel. She swept past him as if he were invisible.

He followed her to the sliding door. From there he

was able to admire her grace as she executed a perfect dive into the pool.

It wouldn't be long before they would be at sea. He would chase down his golden dolphin with the aquamarine eyes until she learned she didn't have to be afraid of him and would swim to him willingly.

CHAPTER EIGHT

PIPER'S sisters drove her the short distance to the chapel from the villa. She squirmed all the way in her wedding finery. Up to now she'd been willing to do anything to save the people she loved, but saying vows in front of a priest meant saying vows to God.

What she was about to do was sacred.

Obviously Nic didn't feel the same way since he'd told her they could get an annulment as soon as Lars was caught and the danger was over. Or, they could stay married and he would try to give her a baby.

Like an off balance painting, Piper knew exactly what was wrong with that picture. So it was either offend God, or live with a man who didn't love her.

Nic hadn't been able to do it. He hadn't been able to stay engaged to Nina because his heart wasn't in it.

His heart wasn't in it now, but because of his chivalrous genes, he would forego love in order to pay his debt to Piper for helping him.

It was horrible. All of it.

"You guys? I can't go through with this."

"You have to."

"Yup."

"Who says?"

"We do."

"He doesn't love me."

"What does that have to do with anything?" Olivia

shut off the motor. "If you foul this up now, it could ruin the whole covert operation."

Greer turned in the seat and flashed her a shrewd regard from her violet eyes. "Forget about wiggling out of this and play it like a Duchess."

More emotional blackmail.

"Oh, all right. Let's get this over with."

Her sisters helped her out of the car where they'd parked next to half a dozen others. The girls wore knee-length pale yellow crepe dresses that fluttered in the light breeze.

"You guys look yummy enough to eat. No wonder your husbands never leave you alone."

Olivia's hot blue eyes narrowed. "Just wait till Nic sees *you*."

"He's seen me plenty, and he never wanted me. I've given him dozens of chan—"

"Here you are," Max broke in on them, looking splendid as usual in his black tux. He carried two bouquets of white and yellow roses which he handed to her sisters.

Luc was right behind him, dashing as always in his tux. He lay the breathtaking sheaf of yellow roses in her left arm. "Nic was starting to get nervous and asked us to come and find you."

"Nervous my eye," she whispered when he kissed her cheek. "You and Max can cut the act around me. I'm here as planned. Let's get the deed done."

He ignored her comments to join his wife.

The tiny chapel overflowed with family and close friends. When the girls started down the aisle on the arms of their husbands, the guests stood up. The absence of music didn't seem to matter.

In fact the hushed silence as everyone stared at the two beautiful in love couples approaching the altar was a sermon in itself.

Piper looked down to make sure both sides of her floor-length mantilla were equal.

They weren't! And it was too late to fix her veil now.

Oh well...

She started walking down the aisle and could imagine everyone twittering at the sight of the lopsided Pastrana bride wearing the Parma pearl. What a fraud she was. For two cents she would run away.

But when she took in the picture of all their loved ones and remembered that she'd agreed to this deception to save lives, her legs carried her to Nic's side.

He stood to the right of the priest, resplendent in a formal black tux with a yellow rose in his lapel.

She thought he might look at her, but he was staring straight ahead, his head and body erect like a prince, his hands clasped in front of him much as if he were awaiting his doom.

Pain ripped through Piper's heart.

The old priest lifted his hands, signaling that everyone should be seated.

In excellent English he said, "I baptized Nicolas soon after he was born. Over the years I've watched him grow and develop into a fine man any parent would be proud of.

"I admit to being curious about the woman he would eventually choose to marry. Nicolas has many rare and unique qualities. But there's a particularly strong adventurous streak in him he shares with his cousins whom I know equally well. It has gotten them into many a scrape.

"So it doesn't surprise me that the three of them ended up choosing a set of unique American triplets to match their indomitable spirits and be their eternal companions.

"Because Nicolas has never been one to leave anything to chance, it doesn't surprise me he has already claimed his bride in a civil wedding in New York.

"Piper Duchess Pastrana, for a man to marry you twice in the same week says something about the depth of his love for you. I'm sorry your parents aren't here today to see you enter into this marriage with Nicolas. But I'm sure they're here in spirit to help bless your union.

"If your sister will take your flowers."

Greer stood closest. She lifted the roses out of her arms.

"Nicolas, please take your bride by the hand."

He grasped it, sending a burning sensation up her arm and through her body.

"Piper, your husband has asked that I perform the actual ceremony in Latin. It has special meaning for him. Though he's too modest to say anything, it pleases me to praise him as one of Andalusia's great scholars. All you have to do is say yes when I pause."

The ceremony began. Piper didn't even know if there was a part in it where she promised to obey her husband or not. It didn't matter because it was a bunch of Latin gobbledygook, and would be annulled in short order.

While her mind wandered in directions that haunted

her, she became aware that the priest had stopped talking. He'd come to the famous pause!

"Yes—" she blurted.

The priest said a few more words which she'd heard often enough to know signaled that they were now man and wife.

For the first time since she'd entered the chapel, Nic turned and looked at her. His piercing brown eyes startled her.

"I love you," he said loud enough for everyone to hear, then he lowered his head and kissed her gently on the lips.

"Do you love me?" he asked out loud after raising up again.

What?

How could he do this to her in front of all these people? What was going on? A last funny prank for the priest's amusement? She knew her face had gone beet red.

"Yes," she whispered.

The priest chuckled on cue.

"I want to hear you say it in front of God and all our family and friends. My bride's a little shy in front of people," he told their guests. "She forgot to give me my ring."

"Oh—"

She took it off her finger and pushed it onto his ring finger. The only way to get out of this was to do his bidding. "I love you, Nic."

He smiled with his eyes as well as his lips. "That wasn't so hard, was it?" In the next breath he gave her a husband's kiss. The kind that went on and on.

When he finally let her go, everyone converged to

congratulate them. The priest pecked her cheek first and told her he was looking forward to baptizing their babies. "Nic's not getting any younger," he winked.

While she was still staggering from that comment, Nic's parents descended on them. His father unbent enough to kiss her on both cheeks and welcome her to the family. Then came her sisters, followed by the parents of her brothers-in-law, Max's married sister and her husband, Luc's brother Cesar and the Robles family.

A photographer snapped pictures as they exited the chapel doors. For a good twenty minutes they posed in different family groupings to preserve this day on film for posterity.

When she felt Olivia's arms go around her she said, "To make this look real, I won't be able to see you and Greer until tomorrow morning."

"Got it. I'll tell Greer. Max took her back to the villa."

"How come?"

"She complained about feeling nauseous. You know how she gets around scented candles."

"I didn't notice any scent except from the flowers."

"I don't know. After the last picture she said she felt faint."

"The poor thing."

"Max hustled her into the car like a shot, insisting she needed to lie down."

"That's good."

Piper felt a strong arm go around her waist. It was Luc. "Come on you two and break this up. Your husband is in the car waiting for the honeymoon to start. I promised I'd bring you to him."

Honeymoon… Right…

With Luc's help, she got in the front seat of Nic's sedan, dress, veil and all. He shut the door and Nic drove them away.

She felt weird. Nervous. A little afraid of Nic.

It was a completely different feeling from before when they'd left Mr. Carlson's office after their first ceremony.

"I saw you huddled with your cousins. Any news about Lars?"

"No one's heard from Signore Barzini yet."

Piper didn't like the situation at all. "Where are we going to spend the night?"

"Someplace totally private."

"I have to go back to the villa to change out of my wedding dress."

"As soon as we reach our destination, we'll both get changed."

The twilight had melted into darkness. She expected to see the lights of the villa appear through the lush foliage any second now. They started down a slope. She remembered descending this road once before. Two more curves and they'd arrived at Nic's private pier.

Her heart almost shot out of its chest cavity to see the *Olivier* tied up to the dock. Luc's sailboat!

"When did that arrive?" she cried. But Nic hadn't heard her because he'd already stopped the car and had come around to help her out.

She refused to move. "I'm not going on that boat."

In the near darkness, the slant of Nic's white smile increased her restiveness. "We don't have a choice, *mi amor.* Signore Barzini wanted everyone off the estate once the ceremony was over.

"Don't forget you and I are supposed to be leaving on our honeymoon. Luc offered his boat which served him and Olivia perfectly well." There was that word honeymoon again. "It's the best way for security to keep close tabs on us."

Even though she couldn't fault his logic, she still shivered. "What about our families?"

"Max and Luc are hosting a dinner at the Las Palmas in Marbella for everyone who attended the wedding. The entire estate is now closed off to anyone except law enforcement officials."

Caught in a tangle of peau-de-soie and lace, she could scarcely see to move. When he reached inside to help her, she tried to swing her legs to the ground. But Nic had a different agenda from hers and picked her up fully in his arms.

Trembling from the incredible feel of being crushed against his solid frame she cried, "Put me down, Nic!"

His tall, powerful body just kept walking. "Not until I've carried my bride over the threshold."

He started across the beach with the hem of her mantilla fluttering in the light breeze. His long strides jostled her, causing her lips to brush against his cheek. Her head reared back as if she'd been stung.

"This is absurd. We don't have an audience now."

"That's true, but we need to put out to sea as soon as possible. Lovely as your wedding finery is, it'll impede your progress if you try to walk across the sand."

Nic always had a reasonable comeback for everything.

Locked in his strong arms, she had no choice but to let him carry her aboard the *Olivier* and deposit her in the tiny, dimly-lit cabin below.

The sight of two bunk beds with their suitcases placed on top of the covers should have been reassuring, but according to Olivia, the sleeping arrangements only added to the excitement of her honeymoon with Luc.

After planting a brief kiss on Piper's lips, Nic undid the buttons of her dress with unexpected speed and proficiency. "Join me on deck when you're ready."

He took the stairs two at a time and disappeared.

Already trembling from a surfeit of emotions, the brief contact of his lips and fingers against her skin had set her on fire. In a daze, she took the few steps to reach her luggage sitting on the bottom bunk.

Either Nic or her sisters had packed an assortment of clothes for her. After removing her wedding dress and mantilla, she found a pair of gray sweats.

While she'd changed into them, Nic had cast off and started the engine. Panic engulfed her to feel the vibrations through her feet. The two of them were now well and truly alone.

She hung her gown in the narrow closet. Once she'd put her white sandals on the shelf, she donned her sneakers and headed for the upper deck. At this point Nic ought to know if Lars and his cronies had ventured into the trap set for them.

The news that the killer had been caught would mean she could go straight to Malaga and fly back to New York on the next plane home.

Piper found Nic at the tiller, framed by the receding lights of the Marbella coastline. Minus his tux jacket and vest, he looked spectacular in his elegant white dress shirt open at the neck, sleeves pushed up to the elbows.

The breeze had grown stronger away from the protection of the inlet. It disheveled his dark brown hair, giving him a slightly dangerous air as the boat began to ride bigger swells.

Her mouth went dry from desire.

The urge to crawl into his lap and wrap her arms around his neck came close to overpowering her.

His gaze trapped hers before she could look away. "I already know the question you're going to ask. The answer is, Lars didn't take advantage of the opportunity we afforded him tonight."

The news confused Piper's emotions. She was frustrated on the one hand to have to continue with this charade, and overjoyed on the other because she couldn't bear to leave Nic.

"Furthermore, the police have checked out the *Britannia* and he's not on board. It's owned by a Hong Kong businessman with an all British crew. It may be that one of them is part of the gang of thugs Lars was making contact with. The authorities are running a thorough background check. They'll eventually come up with some kind of link."

Piper shook her head. "How could Lars have disappeared so easily? He was right in front of us!"

Nic flicked her an enigmatic glance. "That's why we need information only Camilla can feed us. Next week you can go to work on her one way or another."

That left three or four days unaccounted for. Her breathing grew shallow. "And in the meantime?"

"We'll enjoy our honeymoon," he answered in a suave tone.

"I'd rather go back to New York until I have to be a spy."

"That's fine with me. You can show me around your old haunts."

He forced her to count to ten. "I meant alone! I have business to attend to."

"Then I'll come to the office and help you."

Piper decided enough was enough. "Today I told my sisters the real reason why I married you."

Except for the narrowing of his eyelids, Nic's long, hard body didn't move a muscle. If he was angry, he kept it well hidden.

"So," she continued when he didn't say anything, "we don't have to pretend to be the lovesick honeymooners for their sakes."

"We do for my father's sake," he responded in a quiet voice. "It may interest you to know he threatened to renounce me earlier today."

Renounce—

She hugged her arms to her waist, horrified by the revelation. "But he came to the ceremony— He even kissed me on the cheek!"

"Did I ever mention that my father's a master chess player?"

"Nic—" she cried. "He didn't really tell you he didn't want you to be his son anymore, did he?"

His expression turned grim. "He ordered me to give you up. I said I couldn't do that, so he told me not to return to the estate."

Piper felt sick to her stomach, and it wasn't because of the waves. "Then you need to tell him the truth of everything so he'll understand what's really at stake here!''

"If I do that, I'll jeopardize the entire investigation Signore Barzini has set in place. Papa is counting on my not following through with a honeymoon because he can't conceive of my daring to go against his edict.''

She clung to the boat railing to steady herself. "But if you don't have a home to come home to—''

"I own other properties. There's a small villa in Ronda I'm particularly fond of. I keep horses there. It's a short distance from Marbella. When we get back from Vernazza, we'll live there.''

Her head jerked around in his direction. "Vernazza?''

"We'll sail there. Luc tells me the weather is unseasonably warm for February along the Cote D'Azur. Since you never did get to enjoy your Riviera trip on the *Piccione*, we'll do the itinerary you and your sisters planned, only in reverse.''

"But—''

"It's my wedding present to you for helping us,'' he spoke over her protest. "Already you've accomplished something no amount of undercover agents have been able to do. You spotted Lars with Camilla today. That proves the link and has provided the vital break in the case we've been looking for.''

He studied her features as if he could see into her soul. She looked away.

"It's been a long day, Piper. You must be tired. There's food below. After you've eaten, go to bed and sleep. Tomorrow when you awaken, we'll be in St. Tropez where it's much warmer than it is here.

"There's a nice little beach called the Plage des Graniers where we can anchor for the day and enjoy ourselves."

And Nic would be able to sleep.

For them to go on a honeymoon that wasn't really a honeymoon was killing her. "How long do you plan for us to be away?"

"Four days. Once we've flown back to Malaga and get settled at our new home in Ronda, we'll pay a visit to the Robles' villa. Word will reach Papa that I've returned with my bride. It will be up to him if he refuses to ever speak my name again."

Piper trembled in agony for him. "That's horrible!"

"Don't worry about it. This day has been coming since the time I was old enough to realize my father intended that I marry Nina."

"H-how old was that?"

"Ten."

Ten...

"How old was Nina?"

"Seven."

"That long ago?" She shuddered. "How could a father do that to his child?"

"It happens."

His wounds had become hers.

"The sooner we get an annulment, the sooner you'll have the freedom you deserve. You've exchanged one marriage of convenience for another. After what you've just told me, I'll try my hardest to work on Camilla and learn what I can."

"You do that," he murmured.

With the ease of years of practice, he shut off the motor and moved over to the mast where he unfurled the sail. The breeze filled it, causing the boat to lunge forward in a northeasterly direction.

He didn't ask her to linger. She had an idea his thoughts were centered on that moment when he would no longer be in bondage to anyone.

Pain almost incapacitated her on the way down to the cabin.

The prevailing wind cooperated with Nic's agenda. By sunup he could spot the yellow top of St. Tropez's clock tower in the distance. He sailed past the quayside lined with yachts to reach the beach west of the resort.

No sooner did he put in anchor than Piper appeared on deck in jeans and a cotton top that revealed the enticing mold of her body. From the very first moment he'd seen her climb aboard the *Piccione* last June, her golden beauty—those shimmering eyes the same hue as the surrounding aqua waters of Vernazza—had captivated him.

He loved the sound of his adorable wife calling him to breakfast. His performance last night had produced the results he'd been hoping for. In her deep compassion for his pain, she hadn't tried to talk him out of their honeymoon. Instead she'd disappeared below deck and hadn't shown her face until just now.

No matter how much he wanted Lars caught, a part of him couldn't be sorry that he had an excuse to prolong his time alone with Piper. It was the time he needed to persuade her she was in love with him. She had to be. The signs were there. He refused to believe anything else.

"Luc told me Olivia was a gourmet cook. I didn't know you were too."

While they sat at the pull-down table in the tiny galley, Piper poured him another cup of coffee. "Everything you're eating is something she prepared and stocked in the fridge for us. I just warmed it up."

"It tastes good. I'm starving."

"After a night of sailing, I'm not surprised. You must have worked hard out there. You've grown a beard."

His senses ignited. The personal comment proved she'd been studying him beneath those long, feminine eyelashes.

"I promise to shave after I've had a third helping of those lemon crepes."

"They *are* good. Olivia surpassed herself."

"When you consider she's been suffering from morning sickness, her contribution is even more remarkable."

Still avoiding his gaze she said, "After seeing how miserable Olivia gets, Greer said she's glad that she and Max are adopting."

He ate the last crepe sitting on the serving plate. After debating whether he should tell her or not he finally said, "Do you want to know a secret?"

Her head shot up. Those gorgeous eyes were on fire with excitement. "Is she going to be getting her baby right away?"

"No. Max has changed his mind about adopting. At least for a while."

Her happy expression vanished. "You mean Greer doesn't know?" her voice shook.

"Not yet."

''But that's not fair to her!''

Nic covered her hand so she wouldn't slip away. ''On the contrary. About the same time they put in adoption papers, he had his yearly physical. The doctor found out Max had recently married and suggested they do a sperm count to see if it was still as low as it has been since his spleen injury years ago.

''To Max's shock, the count was way up. Another test was done to be certain. It seems that the miraculous ability of the body to heal has turned things around for Max. The doctor sees no reason why they can't get pregnant unless there's a problem with Greer.''

''You're kidding!''

''No…but he doesn't want her to know because the doctor warned him that if she found out, she might focus too much on trying to get pregnant and reduce her ability to conceive.''

''Then she could even be pregnant right now and doesn't know it!''

''That's what Max is hoping.'' He squeezed her fingers before letting her go.

''Oh my gosh—maybe that's the reason she felt sick at the church!''

Nic leaned forward. ''Did your mother suffer from morning sickness?''

His wife stared at him in astonishment. ''Yes! She said the first three months were awful. Then it went away.''

Nic grinned. ''Since the Duchess triplets have so much in common genetically, I wouldn't be surprised if your big sister is going to give Max the baby he's always longed for.''

She bit her lip. "Believing he could never be a biological father must have been hard for him to live with."

"It was." Nic drew in a deep breath. "When he found out, it changed him. The idea of marriage wasn't as appealing. Since I'd always planned to put off my marriage to Nina for as long as possible, the two of us made quite a pair. Things went from bad to worse when Lucas declared he was through with women after he believed his brother had slept with his fiancée.

"At our lowest ebb, who should come along but the Duchess triplets. No one's been the same since. Why don't you come to bed with me, *amorada*. You're a very desirable woman. I would like to consummate our marriage.

"If you want, we could try to make it an even three babies, give or take a few months. Between the six of us, we'll create a new family line…The House of Duchesse-Parma-Bourbon." He got to his feet. "Think about it while I get rid of these whiskers."

CHAPTER NINE

IT WAS a good thing the dishes were unbreakable or Piper would have been forced to buy a whole new set for the galley.

The possibility that Greer could be pregnant should have taken precedence over every other consideration. Yet the only thing Piper could think about was her husband who'd gone to bed after being up all night.

He'd already told her he was in love with someone else. But Piper was the woman he'd married, and just now he'd asked her to join him. All she had to do was take the few steps from the galley to the cabin. She could finally lie in his arms and pour out her love on him until Lars was behind bars.

Why not?

She was tired of the struggle. It really didn't matter whether their marriage ended in an annulment or a divorce. Nic would go his way. She would go hers. Not all the Duchess triplets were destined for husbands and a family. Loving Nic made it impossible to love anyone else. At least she would have this one night for a memory.

With her mind made up, she went in search of him.

He lay on the top bunk in the bottom half of a pair of sweats and nothing else. When she entered the cabin, his head turned toward the doorway. After sailing the boat all night, no wonder his brown eyes looked slightly glazed. He raised up on one elbow.

"Shall I come down, or do you want to come up?" he asked in low, husky voice.

"First we have to discuss something."

The smile he flashed liquified her insides. "Go ahead."

"I don't want to get pregnant, so we would have to take precautions."

"Why?" he fired so fast it stunned her.

"You *know* why."

After a silence, "If that were true, I wouldn't have asked."

"Because after our divorce I don't plan to see you again unless it's at a family gathering once a year or so."

A shadow crossed over his arresting features. He scrutinized her for a tension-filled moment. "Even if we take precautions, there's no guarantee I won't make you pregnant. Since you've given me your bottom line, then I don't dare touch you. A baby needs two parents who love each other.

"Wake me at three, *mi esposa*. By then the temperature should be up around the mid-sixties and we'll be able to take a swim together."

Last year Nic had rejected her with the ostensible excuse he was in official mourning. Just now he'd pushed her away by finding a loophole she couldn't argue with.

"While you sleep, I'm going to do a little sightseeing."

"The town is charming. You can enjoy yourself knowing you're not alone."

He turned on his other side, indicating this conversation had come to an end.

Piper gathered her purse and left the cabin wondering how she could still function considering she was in so much pain. On a scale of one to ten, ten being the worst, her pain registered in the thousands.

Nic had brought the sailboat near enough to shore that she could roll up her jeans and walk onto the beach without getting her clothes wet.

She carried her sneakers. Once her feet and legs were dry, she brushed off the sand, slipped into her shoes and took off for the town center.

It was an odd feeling to know she was being followed, that someone had been watching out for her and Nic from the time they'd arrived in Nice. Undoubtedly it required several dozen different men who alternated shifts.

She didn't even want to think about the expense involved, but had to admit that no matter how deeply Nic had wounded her just now, she was glad he too was being watched and could sleep in safety while she was gone.

After exploring St. Tropez's delightful walkways, she spent several hours in the Annonciade museum studying the paintings of Bonnard, Signac, Dufy, Utrillo and her favorite, Matisse.

By the time she left, the desire to do some sketching of her own prompted her to buy a drawing pad. She revisited a few choice spots to transfer images to paper, then lost track of time capturing scenes at the Place aux Herbes filled with flower and fruit vendors.

When Nic suddenly entered her line of vision looking fantastic in a brown sport shirt and white cargo pants, she let out a small gasp and glanced at her watch. She couldn't believe it was after five o'clock.

Her pulse raced. She jumped up from the bench. "I'm sorry. I forgot the time."

He reached for the pad and leafed through it. "All is forgiven. These sketches are superb." His searching gaze roved over her features. "I'm hungry. Are you?"

She could hardly breathe. "Yes."

"There's a wonderful little restaurant on the waterfront I know you'll enjoy. Shall we go?"

Tucking her purse under one arm, and her drawing pad under the other, she walked with him through the picturesque alleys to their destination.

Throughout their seafood meal she noticed the envious glances the female population gave her when they weren't feasting their eyes on him. Nic appeared oblivious as they made desultory conversation.

By the time they returned to the *Olivier,* night had fallen, lowering the temperature. It was too late for her to want to swim. Not so for Nic who changed into his swimsuit.

While she could hear him splashing about, she got ready for bed and climbed in the bottom bunk. More tired than she realized, she fell asleep before he came in.

When she awakened the next morning, she felt the gentle rocking of the boat. They were at sea again.

She got up to shower and put on a clean pair of jeans and a T-shirt. To her surprise she didn't need a jacket when she joined him on deck. The prevailing warmer trend made it possible for her to enjoy the sun, even with the breeze.

Nic was wearing a pair of cutoffs and a crewneck shirt. He'd donned a pair of sunglasses which made it difficult to assess his mood.

"Any news from Signore Barzini?"

"No."

Well, that certainly said it all. "Where are we headed today?"

"We can put in at any port you like, but the further east we go, the warmer it will be. The decision is up to you."

She took back her assessment of him. He was in a definite mood. Aloof, bordering remote.

"When my sisters and I were planning our trip, Greer listed Alassio as one of the places we should visit."

He nodded. "Excellent choice. It has a white sandy beach and scenic nooks you can sketch to your heart's desire."

In frustration, she rubbed her palms against her hips. "Would you like to go there?"

"Of course."

There was no of course about it. "Have you had breakfast yet?"

"Yes. I would have asked you to join me, but you were sleeping so soundly, I decided it would be criminal to disturb you."

His civility made her feel dismissed. "I'll go eat then."

He said nothing in response.

She disappeared below. Though she had little appetite at this point, she did grab a fresh plum. Before going on deck again, she poured him a cup of coffee for a peace offering. There were several more days to get through. It was going to be agony if this cold war continued.

"Thank you," he murmured minutes later when she handed him a mug of the steaming brew.

"You're welcome."

He clearly wished to be left alone.

She walked to the bow and sank down on one of the banquettes to take in the view of the magnificent coastline. With an aching heart she absorbed the sights and smells, the sheer luxury of being at sea with this extraordinary man on the same boat Luc and Olivia had turned into a love nest.

Piper stayed in that position several hours.

Midafternoon she put on her swimsuit and dove into the water lapping Alassio's shore. Nic dropped anchor and joined her. After a refreshing workout she changed so they could go into town and have dinner at a beach-front hotel restaurant. But she was fast learning that being in paradise with the man you loved was much worse than being alone if he didn't love you.

Once back on board, she went straight to bed with a book. She didn't remember his coming to the cabin at all. The next morning was a repeat of the day before. There was no news from Signore Barzini. Nic asked her what she'd like to see next.

Since they were close to the Cinque Terre, she suggested Monterosso, the place where she and her sisters had thought they would swim on their first night aboard the *Piccione*. Instead, they'd been virtually kidnapped by him and his cousins, and hauled into jail from Lerici harbor.

Once Nic set course for it she asked, "Will my cell phone work from here to call the girls?"

"Yes, but I don't want you phoning them."

She bristled. "Why not?"

"Because they might be with the people who would question why you were trying to make contact while on your honeymoon."

"I've seen *you* on the phone."

"Only to Signore Barzini."

The situation was becoming impossible.

"Nic—" she blurted. "You've sailed these waters all your life. This has to be so boring to you."

"Not at all. I love the sea. It's been a busy time at the bank. Before I have to return to work, I'm enjoying this respite. I'm sorry you're not."

"You know I am! But if there's something else you'd like to do…"

"Since you're asking, I'd like to make love to my wife. Aside from that, I have no other needs right now."

Pain pain pain. "Except to be with the woman you love. Tell me the truth." She struggled to keep her voice steady. "Is it Consuela Munoz?"

"No."

"Then is it a married woman?" she asked, unable to stop herself in time.

"Yes."

"So your situation is hopeless."

"It appears to be."

Her hands curled into fists. "When this case is solved and you can get on with your life, at least you'll be able to find someone else."

The line of his sensual mouth curved almost cruelly. "I don't want anyone else."

"Does she feel the same way about you?"

"Yes."

"Then why doesn't she do something about it?"

She noticed his chest rise and fall. "Because I hurt her."

"Was it something unforgivable?"

"If she never comes to me of her own free will, then I guess I'll have my answer."

Piper shook her head in confusion. "But if there's the slightest hope for the two of you, why did you say anything to me about making *our* marriage real?"

His jaw hardened. "Because I'm tired of waiting for my life to begin. The priest spoke the truth when he said I wasn't getting any younger. The real sin of life would be not to have lived it at all, don't you think?"

"Is that how you honestly feel? That you haven't really lived yet?" She was aghast.

"Not in the way my cousins are living now."

Or her sisters who'd never been so happy in their lives.

"According to my psychiatrist, there's no such thing as one true love. He believes there are at least twenty people a person could be in love with who would be right for them. The trick is to meet them.

"Because you were raised to do your duty, you've never had the opportunity to go spouse hunting. The prospect ought to be rather exciting."

On that note Piper took the empty mug from him and went to the galley so he couldn't see how his comment about not wanting anyone else had come as a fresh blow to her already devastated heart.

She stayed below and made beds, then removed her rings to scour the kitchen and bathroom. Anything to keep out of his way until she could tell he'd dropped anchor. Not willing to hang around him and crucify herself any longer, she changed into another pair of jeans and cotton top to go into town.

When she went up on deck again, she found Nic stretched out on a lounge chair with his shirt off, eyes closed to enjoy the sun.

"Nic? I'm going ashore and probably won't be back until this evening."

"You don't want me to tag along?" he asked without opening his eyes to look at her.

"If you'd like to, but I'll probably do more sketching."

"In that case I'll come and find you when I grow bored with my own company."

Bored with his own company.

Bored with his life.

So why not use the last Duchess triplet to help alleviate it?

Thanks but no thanks.

A half hour later Piper reached the medieval part of the village and began to draw. It helped keep her sanity through the daylight hours. Around six she was feeling hungry and decided to stop for some food before returning to the boat.

No sooner did she start down a small winding side street leading toward the harbor than she heard someone call to her. She could have sworn he said Olivia.

"Wait!"

When she looked over her shoulder, she saw a dark blond guy in his mid-twenties coming bounding toward her. "You do not remember me?" he asked with an accent that could be German or Austrian.

"I'm afraid I don't."

"I am Erik." His light blue eyes studied her relentlessly. "I could have sworn you were the blond American woman who played Frisbee with me and my friends on the beach one evening last summer. My friend Lars was very upset when you would not come to the discotheque with us."

Lars?

Piper gulped.

This was the place Olivia had mentioned seeing him. She'd said he'd been with a group of Germans and Croatians. It all fit.

Her heart thudded in apprehension. "Perhaps you're talking about my sister. We look a lot alike. She came to the Cinque Terre last August on the *Gabbiano*."

He smacked his forehead. "That is the name! For many months Lars kept looking for that boat, but never found it."

She shivered. If Luc hadn't changed the name when he'd had it repainted... "This is an amazing coincidence."

"Yes. Is she with you?"

"No. I'm here on business. What about you?"

"My friends and I crew for a boat charter company out of La Spezia. We live here between jobs."

Did this German know Lars was a killer? Maybe Erik was one of the men who helped steal the Marie-Louise collection. It was possible Lars lived here too. She needed to find out as much as she could.

"You live in paradise."

He smiled. "We think so too. What kind of work brings you to Monterosso?"

"I'm an artist. My paintings appear on calendars in the States."

His gaze wandered to her sketch pad. "Do I get a look?"

"If you'd like." She handed it to him.

After sifting through the pages, he whistled. "You are a genius. The money must be good."

"It's doing better all the time, thank you."

"You have not told me your name yet."

She noticed he hadn't mastered the art of making English contractions.

"It's Piper."

"Like the instrument?"

"Yes."

After he handed it back to her, she started walking toward the harbor. He stuck with her. She felt his eyes assessing her.

"How long will you be in Monterosso?"

Piper didn't want to appear too eager to get to know him. Yet she didn't dare let him find out the *Gabbiano* had undergone a facelift and was anchored off shore.

By now the security man following her should have contacted Nic to tell him she'd been held up by a stranger.

Improvising quickly she said, "I'm taking the train to Portofino 'tonight where I'm booked at the Splendido."

"Nice place. But why not stay over here? I could show you a good time."

"That sounds fun, but I want to get photos of Portofino harbor at first light, then do a full day of sketching. It means an early night for me."

"Then how about tomorrow night? I will tell Lars to bring a girlfriend. The four of us will party."

The hairs stood up on the back of her neck. "I like

the sound of that. Why don't you meet me at the Splendido's pool around seven.''

They'd reached the train station. Erik put his hand on the back of her waist to usher her inside. The uninvited liberty made her skin crawl.

To her relief the ticket agent told her the train to Portofino would be coming in the next five minutes. Unable to shake him, she had to endure his company all the way out to the platform.

''Afterwards we will join some other friends aboard a private yacht.''

She fought to suppress a shudder. ''That sounds exciting. My work has prevented me from doing much socializing.''

''Then I will have to make certain it is memorable.''

There was no mistaking what he meant. The train didn't pull into the station any too soon for her.

''See you tomorrow evening, Erik,'' she said, breaking away from him to climb the steps ahead of several people.

''*Cíao*, Piper.''

She found a seat inside the compartment. He stood outside the window and smiled at her, forcing her to wave back at him. The second the train left the station, she whipped out her cell phone.

With trembling hands, she phoned Nic. He answered before the second ring. ''Your security guard watched you get on the train. Are you all right, *mi amor?*'' he demanded without preamble.

The concern in his deep voice, plus the knowledge that he'd followed her inside the station was something to treasure. ''I'm fine.''

''Thank God for that! Who was the man?''

She clutched the phone tighter. "His name is Erik. He was one of the guys with Lars when Olivia happened to join them for a game of Frisbee last August. He mistook me for her.

"I've set up a double date for the four of us tomorrow night at the Splendido. That's where I'm going now. I found out they crew for a company from La Spezia."

When she didn't hear anything back, it dawned on her the train had already started through the tunnels. No telling at what point her words had broken up.

By the time she reached Portofino, the service was working again, but Nic didn't answer. She imagined he'd gone back to the *Olivier* and would call the second he could.

But in that assumption she was wrong. When she'd checked into the fabulous hotel a half hour later where she'd once stayed with Greer and Olivia, she still hadn't heard from him. In case Erik or Lars asked questions of the concierge tomorrow evening, she used her credit card with her maiden name so they wouldn't be able to associate her with Nic.

Another half hour went by without a call from him.

Unable to stop pacing, yet afraid to go out again, she rang for room service and ordered dinner.

One hour turned into two, then three. She lay on top of the bed and watched Italian TV while she waited to hear from him.

At midnight she couldn't stand it any longer and phoned Greer even though Nic had warned her not to call anyone because they were supposed to be on their honeymoon.

All Piper got was her sister's voice mail. The same

thing happened when she phoned Olivia. In desperation she called her brothers-in-law's cell phones, but was met with more instructions to leave a message.

For no one to be available meant something vital was going on. To her chagrin, everyone knew about it except her!

When her cell phone finally rang, she almost jumped out of her skin. ''Nic?'' she cried out.

''No, it's Greer. I'm calling from home. Olivia's on the other extension.''

Piper got up from the bed. ''Thank heaven you guys called me back! I'm in a hotel room at the Splendido dying to know what's going on. While I was telling Nic that I'd found Lars, we lost phone contact. If anything bad has happened to him I wouldn't want to go on liv—''

''Piper!'' her sister interrupted. ''Listen to me. Max just phoned from police headquarters in Rome. Luc and Nic are with him and Signore Barzini. Your husband is fine! Everyone is safe and everything's wonderful!''

''It's true!'' Olivia chimed in. ''Thanks to the information you gave him, Lars and Erik were picked up by the police earlier tonight. They're in custody along with another member of the crew from the *Britannia*.''

''You're kidding! It's over?''

''Yes! Everything!''

''Oh you guys— I can't believe it!'' Tears gushed down her cheeks.

''We're so proud of you. We're in awe of your courage.''

''Courage had nothing to do with it, Olivia. Once I

realized what was happening, I just played along until I could get Nic on the phone.''

"According to Max that isn't how Nic tells the story,'' Greer said. "Unfortunately they're all in a debriefing right now. Nic left strict instructions for you to stay put and pamper yourself until he gets there.

"With Max being the legal counsel for the family, there's a lot of business that will take our husbands all night to sort out. Besides the matter of the rest of the missing jewels, there's the human side to this.

"Nic's parents along with Camilla and the Robles family were summoned to Rome. They're hearing about Nina's murder right now.''

Piper sank down on the edge of the bed. "How awful for them.''

"Absolutely,'' Olivia commiserated, "but at least we know the killers have been caught.''

The news that all the people Piper loved were no longer in danger filled with her with joy. But now there was a new problem, one she hadn't thought she would have to face this soon.

"Piper? Are you still there?''

"Yes. I guess I'm still in shock that this whole thing is really over.''

"We know what you mean. Hard to believe we were once suspects.''

Piper let out a mirthless laugh. "That seems a century ago.''

"Makes you believe it was destiny that brought us to Europe in the first place, doesn't it?'' Olivia said. Destiny for everyone except Piper. "And now we're married to the most wonderful husbands in the world.''

"We are," Piper whispered.

"You sound odd," Greer observed. "I think we'd better come and keep you company."

"No!" No. "That's very sweet of you guys, but it's the middle of the night and I'm exhausted. I'm sure you are too."

"No one's going to sleep tonight. We're on our way."

"But—"

"You did the 'one for all' part earlier tonight. Now we're going to the 'all for one' part for you!" Greer declared in a no-nonsense voice. "See you in an hour."

Piper couldn't hang up fast enough. A chill had permeated her body because the realization that the case was solved meant she no longer had a reason to stay with Nic.

If she left for New York right now, their annulment could go through without a hitch and he'd be free to find someone to love. Perhaps not the great love of his life, but at least it would be a woman he could choose without any strings attached.

Ten minutes later she asked the taxi driver to head for the Genoa airport.

At three-thirty in the morning Nic's cell phone rang. He excused himself from the briefing with the Robles family and went out in the hall to take the call. Since all the relatives were assembled in Rome except for Piper's sisters, no one but his wife would be calling him.

Needing to hear her voice, he clicked on without checking the Caller ID. "Piper?"

"Pardon, Señor de Pastrana. This is Signore Galli, the head of security at Genoa airport. We have detained one of the Duchess triplets trying to board a flight to New York."

Nic groaned.

"When we asked her the nature of her business in Italy this time, she refused to tell us anything, so I'm holding her. She has no jewelry on her, only a drawing pad and her purse. We took her cell phone away from her of course.

"Now she's demanding the right to call her attorney in New York. I told her I would allow it as soon as she gave us the information we desired. At that point she insisted that she was *your* wife, *Señor,* that you would clear this up so she could take her flight home."

Her home is with me.

"You did the right thing, Signore Galli. Where have you put her?"

"In the detention room."

"Very good. Make sure she has a cot, a warm blanket and any food or drinks she would like."

"Of course."

"Under no circumstances are you to allow her sisters in to see her or talk to her."

"*Sí, Señor.*"

"I probably can't be there for another hour or two. One more thing—let her have her drawing pad and purse. She's an artist and will be happier if she has something to do."

"*Capische.*"

He'd no sooner hung up than Luc asked, "What's going on with Piper?"

Nic hadn't realized his cousin was standing behind

him. "She tried to leave for New York. Signore Galli has detained her at the Genoa airport."

Luc studied him for a long moment. "You didn't tell her the real reason why you wanted to marry her, so why look so shocked now? You knew this day had to come.

"You and Uncle Carlos are a lot alike. You both have too much Pastrana pride. It's that damnable pride that keeps you both from opening up.

"Deep down Uncle Carlos loves you and wants your love. But he can't bring himself to tell you he didn't mean it about renouncing you because he's afraid he won't hear the right answer back."

"You think I don't know that?"

"Do you?" Luc challenged. "Then how come you've frozen Piper out the same way?"

Luc didn't know it, but he was preaching to the converted. Filling his lungs with air Nic said, "I gave Papa the right answer a few minutes ago even though he wasn't asking for it.

"The moment was sobering for both of us. He broke down sobbing and begged my forgiveness. We embraced like we should have been doing for years."

"I'm glad to hear it," Luc said in a husky tone.

"As for Piper—" Nic cleared his throat. "You're right about everything you said. Last year I had to reject her for all the obvious reasons, yet I expected her to understand and love me anyway.

"When she fought me so hard, I was terrified that I might have wounded her beyond repair, so I haven't allowed her to see into my heart. It's no wonder she's trying to leave me, but I won't let it happen. The old

Nic is gone, Luc. The new one is on his way to Genoa to grovel if that's what it takes.''

"I hate to tell you this, *mon vieux,* but it will.''

A shudder rocked Nic's body. "I can't lose her. She's my life, Luc! Make my excuses to Signore Barzini. Tell him something more important than this case has cropped up and has to be dealt with immediately. My whole existence depends on it.''

"I know exactly how you feel. When I set up that business with Signore Tozetti to get Olivia back to Europe, I was shaking in my proverbial boots.''

"I'm shaking in mine. Tell Max I'll phone him on my way to the plane and let him know what's going on.''

"It'll be an enormous relief to him.''

"I realize that,'' Nic murmured. "When it comes to Piper, the girls are like mother lionesses defending their cub. I'm sure their worry over her hasn't made it easy for either of you.''

Luc flashed him that old, familiar Falcon smile. "Fix the problem and we'll forgive everything.''

"I intend to.''

CHAPTER TEN

IT WAS only five in the morning. Piper had been lying there in the dark, sick at heart. She'd expected to have to wait another twelve hours before Nic showed up in the windowless room where she was being detained.

He turned on the light. It prompted her to pull the blanket over her head in order to shut out his handsome features.

She heard the legs of the chair scrape the floor as he approached the cot.

"I didn't have any idea Signore Galli was going to detain you, Piper. I swear it!"

"Please turn out the light. It hurts my eyes."

In the next moment all went dark.

"Is that better?" he asked in a gravelly voice. She could tell he was sitting next to her again.

"Much."

"The last time you girls tried to leave Italy, he was given orders to detain you. We told him we believed you were being used to take the real jewels out of the country. He had no way of knowing everything has changed since last June."

Hot tears trickled from her eyes. "He does his job well. As Mr. Carlson once said, the Italians may have an unorthodox system, but it works."

"It does... It did in your case, thank God," his voice shook.

"Once again you've accomplished your objective by preventing me from leaving the country."

"I'm not talking about that, Piper. I would have come after you and found you wherever you went. I'm talking about the police catching Lars in the corridor of the Splendido outside your door. He knocked your security guard unconscious and was about to break in on you."

Her body turned to ice. "Lars was in the hall?" her voice shook.

"Yes. After your phone call, I alerted the police and followed Erik to a pensione near the station. In a few minutes I saw Lars leave by car and knew in my gut he was headed for the Splendido.

"After the police raided the pensione, Erik was flown to Rome along with another sailor who crewed for the *Britannia*. I took the helicopter to Portofino. But there was a delay at takeoff due to a mechanical problem. By the time I reached the Splendido, Lars had been apprehended and I was needed in Rome."

She shivered and buried her face in the pillow.

"Answer me one question. Why didn't you lead Erik to the boat? Don't you know I would have protected you? Did you have so little faith in your husband?" his voice throbbed.

Piper raised up again. "It wasn't that. Erik thought I was Olivia. When I told him he'd probably met my sister who'd come to Monterosso on the *Gabbiano* last summer, he said something about Lars having tried to find the boat for several months after.

"I was afraid he would see the *Olivier* and notice it was the same boat. What if he alerted Lars and you were given the slip again? So I pretended that I was on a business trip, and took the train everywhere.

"I made up the excuse that I needed to be in Portofino to catch the early morning light. Erik seemed to buy my story and suggested joining me there the next evening. He said he would ask Lars to come and bring a girlfriend along.

"I had no idea if that meant Camilla, but I didn't say anything of course. He revolted me, but I didn't know what else to do."

"Under the circumstances, that was a brilliant maneuver on your part," Nic asserted. "But you put your life in danger to do it."

"I'm glad Lars has been stopped. That's all that's important. Now I can go back to New York and my job."

"No, darling."

She clutched the sheet in her hands. "What did you just call me?"

"What I've been calling you all along in Spanish…my love, my darling, my adorable wife, my beloved, my heart, my soul."

Her eyes smarted. "Please don't, Nic. Enough's enough."

"Agreed. No more masks, no more games. Right now this is just you and me alone at last, with the truth the only thing we've got going for us."

Her brows lifted. "You sound weird."

"That's because you're talking to a broken man."

"The Nicolas de Pastranas of the world don't break."

"That's just a persona I wear so no one can see inside to the real me."

"Be serious, Nic," she said crossly.

"I've never been more serious in my life. I was raised to be a Pastrana through and through. I learned early that as long as I conformed to my father's vision for me, I could have anything I wanted, be anything I wanted.

"Money, position, entitlements—it was all there. Having two cousins equally endowed enabled us to live extraordinary lives. I don't ever recall envying another human being until Papa called in the one favor that darkened my world."

"You mean Nina."

"Yes."

"But you told me you knew you would have to marry her from the time you were ten years old."

"That's true, but what I didn't tell you was that I had no intention of carrying out his wishes."

She turned her head in his direction. "Then I don't understand."

"There's only one reason our engagement took place. Papa suffered a mild heart attack, or so my mother and I were informed. While he was recovering, he said he was afraid he was going to die before he saw me married to Nina.

"The doctor took me aside and told me that any undue stress could bring on a fatal attack. It was the one lie I didn't see coming."

Piper was incredulous. "The doctor *lied* to you about your father's condition?"

"Papa made him do it. In reality my father had been rushed to the hospital for acute indigestion after eating too many of his favorite prawns. It masked a heart attack.

"He'd found the perfect excuse he needed to get me to do what he wanted, which was to become officially engaged to Nina and set a wedding date.

"I fell for the oldest ploy in the world, and it worked until the day I asked him how his heart was doing. Had he had a recent checkup? He acted so strangely, I confronted the doctor who couldn't look me in the eye. Then I knew…"

She shot up in the cot. "I can't imagine any father doing that."

"My father's one of a rare breed. When I realized what he'd done, that was the day I put the plan in motion to travel to Cortina and break my engagement to Nina. I knew she wasn't in love with me either, but she was too timid and biddable to dare thwart her autocratic father openly."

"I can't comprehend any of it."

"If I hadn't lived it, I wouldn't be able to comprehend it either, but her secret affair with Lars made perfect sense to me.

"When I told her I couldn't marry her, she tried to hide her joy from me, but I knew that breaking our engagement had made her happy. The great tragedy was that out of all the men Nina could have picked to love, it had to be someone as ruthless as Lars."

By now Piper was trembling with pain for both him and Nina. "How did your father dare let you go into official mourning knowing he'd tricked you into getting engaged?"

"Actually he didn't say or do anything to encourage it."

"What?"

"I knew he felt terrible for what he'd done to me,

and horribly guilty because Nina died. The truth is, the last woman in the world he wanted me to marry was Camilla who didn't have Nina's sweetness. So I purposely went into mourning to let him think he would end up getting a daughter-in-law he didn't want.''

''Nic—''

''I'm a horrible man, Piper, and I'm not proud of my behavior. I did it to pay him out. For myself, I wanted to honor her memory. If I hadn't asked her to marry me, she might not be dead now.''

Piper groaned. ''Neither you, your father or Señor Robles could have known Nina would die because a killer was on the loose.''

''Nevertheless she did die, and I was the person responsible,'' his voice grated.

She bowed her head. ''I'm sorry I didn't take your mourning seriously.''

''Don't you dare apologize for that!'' he muttered fiercely. ''When you girls came aboard the *Piccione,* I fell totally and irreversibly in love with you. It hit so hard and fast, I didn't know myself any longer.

''While love was happening to my cousins, I had to pretend it wasn't happening to me, to us. I owed Nina that year's penance. So I made a secret vow that I wouldn't go near you or touch you until the twelve months had passed.

''Piper—when you reached out to me after Max's wedding, I loathed myself for wanting you so much. I had to be cruel to you. There was no other way to withstand my feelings.

''When you flew to Spain in August and Luc married Olivia, I wanted to make it a double wedding.

That night you have no idea how close I came to kidnapping you from Luc's robot car and forcing you to marry me whether you wanted me or not.''

What Piper was hearing now made her euphoric.

''I'll never know how I let you go, but be assured I was counting the hours until February when I could come to you and beg you to marry me.

''But the second I saw you sitting at your desk, so beautiful, so unapproachable, I lost my nerve because I knew I'd hurt you, possibly beyond your ability to forgive me. I almost did have a heart attack when you told me you'd gotten engaged to Don.

''Even if it had been true, I was like a madman, and would have fought him to the death for you.''

In the next instant Nic had joined her on the cot. He pushed her back down so he was half lying on top of her. ''I'd just learned that Nina had been murdered, and used her once more in my own way, which was to get you to marry me.''

Piper's hands slid to his face where she could feel the beginnings of a beard. ''You didn't need to go that far, my darling. You knew I loved you, that I was yours for the taking,'' she whispered against his lips.

''Say it again, Piper.''

''I love you. I'm in love with you,'' she cried fervently. ''Do you honestly think I would have agreed to your insane suggestion that I spy for you if I hadn't been willing to follow you to the ends of the earth?''

The last was stifled as she felt his mouth close over hers. Though he'd kissed her before, nothing would ever compare to this kiss which filled her with ecstasy and begged her to love him without restraint.

''Nic—'' She fought for breath when he finally relinquished her lips. "We can't do this here. Not the way I feel about you."

His mouth roamed over her features, her neck, her hair, driving her to a feverish pitch. "I know exactly where to go. Come with me, *amorada*."

It was surprising that the lower bunk of the *Olivier* wasn't much wider than the cot at the airport, but over the next four days Piper never noticed where they slept or what they ate.

What mattered was being in Nic's arms and loved beyond comprehension.

"Is there anything you want this morning?" he whispered, biting her earlobe gently the second he woke up.

One thing she'd learned about her new husband. He was so excited and eager about everything, he reminded her of a child who ran downstairs to open the Christmas presents before anyone else was up.

She adored this man who had such a zest for living and loving, it took her breath. He never stopped telling her and showing her how much he desired her.

Right now he was teasing her, giving her little kisses here and there to nudge her awake. Tangled as they were, it wasn't enough. He wanted her attention and he wanted it now.

"I *do* want something this morning."

For that much response he began making love to her in earnest. An hour later she stared into his eyes, so crazy in love with him there were no words.

"As I was saying before you sidetracked me, there is something I want."

"Name it," he whispered against her lips swollen from his kisses.

"We need a sailboat like this. Poor Luc and Olivia have been deprived of theirs long enough."

"I've been thinking the same thing ever since we left Genoa. When we get back to Marbella, we'll go shopping."

Her aqua eyes lit up excitedly. "I can't wait! I know exactly what I want to call it."

"So do I," he said mysteriously.

"But I want the name I've chosen to be on it."

He flashed her what she now referred to as his Andalusian grin. "Mine's better."

"Tell me what it is."

"You first, *mi amor.*"

"The *Don Juan.*"

He chuckled. "I would never allow it. We'll call it the *Golden Dolphin.*"

Though she loved his choice she said, "I like mine better."

"No, Piper."

"I think we're having our first fight."

Nic let out a laugh that started deep in his belly. She loved his laugh. "We've had so many, this one must be number two hundred at least."

"As long as we're always in bed to make up, I'll never mind."

"You're shameless, Señora de Pastrana. I love you." He buried his face in her profusion of gold silk.

"I can't wait to cook our first meal and clean my new house."

"We have a housekeeper and maids to do that."

"How about only employing them on the weekends.

Monday through Friday I want to pretend we're a normal married couple. I need to cook and clean and toil for you.''

The laughter continued to burst forth, reverberating in the tiny cabin. ''Which home do you want to call home?''

She lifted her head. ''What do you mean?''

''Well, there's the one in Marbella, and another one in Ronda.''

''Ronda?'' Piper blinked. ''I've heard about that place way up high in the mountains. We have two homes?'' she squealed.

''*Sí, mi esposa.*'' He kissed the end of her retrousse nose. ''Before my father and I made up in Rome, he'd renounced me and ordered me off the estate for marrying you. I'd made up my mind we would live in Ronda where I have horses.''

Her heart did a little kick. ''You're serious.''

''About the horses? Completely.''

''No—'' she cried, sliding her arms around his neck. ''He actually would have renounced you?''

''The old version of him would have, but after hearing that Nina was murdered, he realized how close he came to losing a nephew too, not to mention his son. So he's had a complete change of heart and we're off on a new footing. The one we should have been on all along.''

''Thank heaven, Nic.''

He nodded. ''Papa admitted that if he were years younger, and he hadn't already met Mother, he would have fought for your hand.''

''You're kidding!''

''No,'' he said, sounding more serious all of a sudden. "He's very taken with the Duchess triplets, especially the artiste of the family."

"I'm so glad you've made up with him, darling!"

"So am I. Otherwise he would have cut himself off from enjoying his grandchildren."

"Oh really— I didn't know he had any," she said with as straight a face as she could muster.

"He might already have three grandchildren, but the golden baby girls are very little, possibly only four days old."

"Girls?" she cried in shock. Not until this moment did she even consider the possibility she could have triplets.

"Yes. Papa will be the envy of every grandfather in Andalusia."

Piper grinned. "And you will be the most haggard, sleep deprived father on the planet. My father never quite survived the ordeal."

"Ah, but I'm a good deal younger than your father when he made your mother pregnant."

"It might be three boys, or a mix."

He crushed her against his body. "I'll take whatever comes with the greatest of joy. You're the love of my life, Piper. I can't believe we're finally together like this with a whole wonderful future to look forward to."

She nestled closer. "Do you want to know a secret?"

"Do you have to ask?"

"When my sisters and I planned our trip to Europe, I was the one who suggested we wear the Duchesse pendants. Just think…if I hadn't ment—"

"Let's not think about it," he broke in on her. "I

don't want to think about it. The thought of not meeting you is like imagining no life after this one, no stars in the heavens, no air to breathe, no lips to kiss, no heart to set on fire. Am I making myself clear?''

''As crystal. Make love to me again and never stop.''

''I was just going to do it, with or without your permission.''

''Oh Nic—''

Harlequin Romance®

Contract Brides

From paper marriage...to wedded bliss?

A wedding dilemma:

What should a sexy, successful bachelor do if he's too busy
making millions to find a wife? Or if he finds the perfect
woman, and just has to strike a bridal bargain...?

The perfect proposal:

The solution? For better, for worse, these grooms in a hurry
have decided to sign, seal and deliver the ultimate
marriage contract...to buy a bride!

Coming soon to

HARLEQUIN®
Romance®

in favorite miniseries Contract Brides:

A WIFE ON PAPER
by award-winning author Liz Fielding, #3837
on sale March 2005

VACANCY: WIFE OF CONVENIENCE
by Jessica Steele, #3839
on sale April 2005

Available wherever Harlequin books are sold.

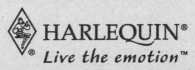

HARLEQUIN®
Live the emotion™

www.eHarlequin.com

HRCB

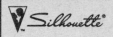
Silhouette®

INTIMATE MOMENTS™

presents a provocative new miniseries by
award-winning author

INGRID WEAVER

PAYBACK

Three rebels were brought back from the brink and
recruited into the shadowy Payback Organization.
In return for this extraordinary second chance, they
must each repay one favor in the future. But if they
renege on their promise, everything that matters
will be ripped away...including love!

Available in March 2005:

The Angel and the Outlaw
(IM #1352)

Hayley Tavistock will do anything to avenge the
murder of her brother—including forming an
uneasy alliance with gruff ex-con Cooper Webb.
With the walls closing in around them, can love
defy the odds?

Watch for Book #2 in June 2005...

Loving the Lone Wolf
(IM #1370)

Available at your favorite retail outlet.

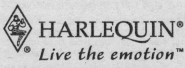